Allan Ramsay

The Tea-table miscellany

A collection of choice songs, Scots and English ..

Allan Ramsay

The Tea-table miscellany
A collection of choice songs, Scots and English ..

ISBN/EAN: 9783741195891

Manufactured in Europe, USA, Canada, Australia, Japa

Cover: Foto ©Andreas Hilbeck / pixelio.de

Manufactured and distributed by brebook publishing software
(www.brebook.com)

Allan Ramsay

The Tea-table miscellany

THE

Tea-Table

MISCELLANY.

Behold, and liften, while the Fair
Breaks in fweet Sounds the willing Air;
And, with her own Breath, fans the Fire
Which her bright Eyes do firft infpire:
What Reafon can that Love controul,
Which more than one Way courts the Soul ?
                            E. Waller

EDINBURGH:
Printed by Mr. Thomas Ruddiman,
for Allan Ramsay, at the Mercury,
oppofite to the Crofs-Well, 1724.

T O

Ilka lovely Britih *Las,*
Frae Ladys Charlote, Anne, *and*
Jean,
Down to ilk bonny singing Bes,
  Wha dances barefoot on the Green;

D EAR LASSES,
  Your most humble Slave,
Wha ne'er to serve ye shall decline;
Kneeling wad your Acceptance crave,
  When he presents this sma' Propine.

THEN take it kindly to your Care,
  Revive it with your tunefu' Notes:
Its Beauties will look sweet and fair,
  Arising safely through your Throats.

THE Wanton wee Thing will rejoice,
  When tensed by a sparkling E·e,
The Spinner tinkling with her Voice,
  Is lying on her lovely Knee.

WHILE Kettles dringe on Ingles durs,
  Or Clashes flays the Lazy Lass,
Thir Sangs may ward you frae the sour,
  And gayly vacant Minutes pass.

E'EN while the Tea's fill'd reeking round,
  Rather than plot a tender Tongue,
Treat a' the circling Lugs wi' Sound,
  Syne safely sip when ye have sung.

MAY Happiness bad up your Hearts,
  And warm ye lang with loving Fires,
May Powers propitious play their Parts
  In matching you to your Desires.
Edinʳ. *January*
  1. .1724.
                    A. RAMSAY.

                          Bonny

Bony *Christy*.

HOW sweetly smells the Summer
green?
Sweet taste the Peach and Cherry;
Painting and Order please our Een,
And Claret makes us merry:
But finest Colours, Fruits and Flowers,
And Wine, tho' I be thirsty,
Lose a' their Charms and weaker Powers,
Compar'd with those of *Christy*.

WHEN wandring o'er the flowry Park,
No nat'ral Beauty wanting;
How lightsome is't to hear the Lark,
And Birds in Consort chanting:

A   But

But if my *Chrifty* tunes her Voice,
   I'm rap't in Admiration,
My Thoughts with Extafies rejoice,
   And drap the hale Creation.

When e'er fhe fmiles a kindly Glance,
   I take the happy Omen,
And aften mint to make Advance, .
   Hoping fhe'll prove a Woman :
But dubious of my ain Defert,
   Me Sentiments I fmother
With fecret Sighs I vex my Heart,
   For Fear fhe love another.

Thus fang blate *Edie* by a Burn,
   His *Chrifty* did o'erhear him,
She doughtna let her Lover mourn,
   But e'er he wift drew near him.
She fpake her Favour with a Look,
   Which left nae Room to doubt her,
He wifely this white Minute took,
   And flang his Arms about her.

My

My *Chrifly!* — witnefs, bony Stream,
   Sic Joys frae Tears arifing,
I wifh this may na be a Dream;
   O Love the maift furprifing!
Time was too precious now for Tauk,
   This Point of a' his Wifhes,
He wadna with fet Speeches bauk,
   But wair'd it a' on Kifles.

The Bufh aboòn Traquhair.

HEAR me, ye Nymphs, and every
               Swain,
   I'll tell how *Peggy* grieves me,
Tho' thus I languifh, thus complain,
   Alas, fhe ne'er believes me.
                  A 2   My.

My Vows and Sighs, like filent Air,
   Unheeded never move her;
At the bony Bufh abuon *Traquair*,
   'Twas there I firft did love her.

That Day fhe fmil'd, and made me glad,
   No Maid feem'd ever kinder,
I thought my felf the luckieft Lad,
   So fweetly there to find her.

I try'd to footh my am'rous Flame,
   In Words that I thought tender,
If more there pafs'd, I'm not to blame,
   I meant not to offend her.

Yet now fhe fcornful flies the Plain,
   The Fields we then frequented,
If e'er we meet, fhe fhews Difdain,
   She looks as ne'er acquainted.

The bony Bufh bloom'd fair in *May*,
   Its Sweets I'll ay remember;
But now her Frowns make it decay,
   It fades, as in *December*.

Y 2

Yᴇ rural Powers, who hear my Strains,
  Why thus should *Peggy* grieve?
Oh! make her Partner in my Pains,
  Then let her Smiles relieve me.
If not, my Love will turn Despair,
  My Passion no more tender;
I'll leave the Bush aboon *Traquair*,
  To lonely Wilds I'll wander.

C.

An ODE

To the Tune of Polwarth *on the Green.*

THo Beauty, like the Rose
  That smiles on *Polwarth* Green,
In various Colours shows,
As 'tis by Fancy seen:

A 3   ¶a

Yet all its different Glories ly
    United in thy Face,
And Virtue, like the Sun on high,
    Gives Rays to ev'ry Grace.

So charming is her Air,
    So smooth, so calm her Mind,
That to some Angel's Care
    Each Motion seems assign'd:
But yet so chearful, sprightly, gay,
    The joyful Moments fly,
As if for Wings they stole the Ray
    She darteth from her Eye.

Kind am'rous Cupids, while
    With tuneful Voice she sings,
Perfume her Breath and smile,
    And wave their balmy Wings:
But as the tender Blushes rise,
    Soft Innocence doth warm,
The Soul in blissful Extasies
    Dissolveth in the Charm.

D.
TWEED.

Tweed-Side.

WHAT Beauties does *Flora* difclofe?
   How fweet are her Smiles upon
      Tweed ?
Yet *Mary's* ftill fweeter than thofe,
   Both Nature and Fancy exceed.
Nor Daifie, nor fweet blufhing Rofe,
   Nor all the gay Flowers of the Field,
Nor *Tweed* gliding gently thro' thofe,
   Such Beauty and Pleafure does yield.

THE Warblers are heard in the Grove,
   The Linnet, the Lark and the Thrufh,
The Black-bird, and fweet cooing Dove,
   With Mufick enchant ev'ry Bufh.
Come let us go forth to the Mead,
   Let us fee how the Primrofes fpring,
We'll lodge in fome Village on *Tweed*,
   And love while the feather'd Folks fing.

A :   H o w

How does my love pass the long Day?
  Does *Mary* not 'tend a few Sheep?
Do they never carelesly stray,
  While happily she lyes asleep?
Tweed's-Murmures should lull her to Rest,
  Kind Nature indulging my Bliss,
To relieve the soft Pains of my Breast,
  I'd steal an ambrosial Kiss.

'Tis she does the Virgins excell,
  No Beauty with her may compare,
Love's Graces all round her do dwell,
  She's fairest, where Thousands are fair.
Say, Charmer, where do thy Flocks stray?
  Oh! tell me at Noon where they feed;
Shall I seek them on sweet winding *Tay*,
  Or the pleasanter Banks of the *Tweed*.

C

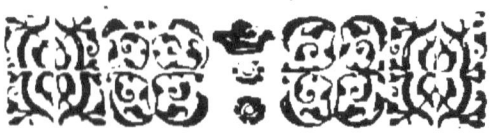

SONG.

To the Tune of, *Wo's my Heart that we should sunder.*

IS *Hamilla* then my own,
    O the Dear, the charming Treasure!
Fortune now in vain shall frown,
All my future Life is Pleasure.

S*ee* how rich with youthful Grace,
Beauty warms her ev'ry Feature;
Smiling Heaven is in her Face,
All is gay, and all is Nature.

S*ee* what mingling Charms arise,
Rosy Smiles and kindling Blushes;
Love sits laughing in her Eyes,
And betrays her secret Wishes.

HASTE

HASTE then from th' *Idalian* Grove,
Infant Smiles, and Sports, and Graces,
Spread the downy Couch for Love,
And lull us in your sweet Embraces.

SOFTEST Raptures, pure from Noise,
This fair happy Night surroud us,
While a Thousand spritly Joys
Silent flutter all around us.

THUS unsowr'd with Care or Strife,
Heaven still guard this dearest Blessing,
While we tread the Path of Life,
Loving still, and still possessing,

S.

A

A
S O N G.

Let's be jovial, fill our Glasses,
  Madness 'tis for us to think,
How the World is rul'd by Asses,
  And the Wise are sway'd by Chink.
Fal la ra, &c.

Then never let vain Cares oppress us,
  Riches are to them a Snare,
We're ev'ry one as rich as *Crœsus,*
  While our Bottle drowns our Care.
Fa la ra, &c,·

              WINE

WINE will make us red as Roses,
  And our Sorrows quite forget,
Come let us fuddle all our Noses,
  Drink ourselves quite out of Debt.
Fa la ra, &c.

WHEN grim Death comes looking for us,
  We are topping at our Bowls,
Bacchus joining in the *Chorus*;
  Death, begone, here's none but Souls.
Fa la ra, &c.

GODLIKE *Bacchus* thus commanding,
  Trembling Death away shall fly,
Ever after understanding
  Drinking Souls can never dy.
Fa la ra, &c.

X.

(13)

Muirland Willie.

HARKEN and I will tell you how
Young Muirland *Willie* came to woo,
Tho he cou'd neither say nor do;
   The Truth I tell to you.
But ay he cries, What e'er betide,
Maggy I'se ha'e her to be my Bride,
With a fal, dal, &c.

  ON his Gray Yad as he did ride,
With Durk and Pistol by his Side,
He prick'd her on wi' mikle Pride,
   Wi' mikle Mirth and Glee.
Out o'er yon Moss, out o'er yon Muir,
Till he came to her Dady's Door,
With a fal dal, &c.

B   GOOD

Goodman, quoth he, be ye within,
I'm come your Doghter's Love to win,
I care no for making meikle Din,
    What Answer gi' ye me?
Now, Woer, quoth he, wou'd ye light
      down,
I'se gie ye my Doghter's Love to win,
With a fal, dal, &c.

    Now, Woer, sin ye are lighted down,
Where do ye win, or in what Town?
I think my Doghter winna gloom
    On sick a Lad as ye.
The Woer he step'd up the House,
And wow but he was wond'rous crouse,
With a fal, &c.

    I have three Owsen in a Plough,
Twa good ga'n Yads, and Gear enough,
The Place they ca' it *Cadeneugh*;   .
    I scorn to tell a Lie:
Besides, I had frae the great Laird,
A Peat-Pat and a Lang-kail Yard,
With a fal, &c.

                       THE

THE Maid pat on her Kirtle brown,
She was the braweſt in a' the Town;
I wat on him ſhe did na gloom,
   But blinkit bonnilie.
The Lover he ſtended up in Haſte,
And gript her hard about the Waſte,
   With a fal, &c.

   To win your Love, Maid, I'm come here;
I'm young, and hae enough o' Gear,
And for my ſell ye need na fear,
   Troth try me whan ye like.
He took aff his Bonnet and ſpat in his Chew,
He dighted his Gab, and he pri'd her Mou'.
With a fal, &c.

   THE Maiden bluſht and bing'd fu' law,
She had na Will to ſay him na,
But to her Dady ſhe left it a',
   As they twa cou'd agree.
The Lover he ga'e her the tither Kiſs,
Syne ran to her Dady and tell'd him this,
With a fal, &c.

Your Doghter wad na say me na,
But to your sell she has left it a',
As we cou'd gree between us twa,
   Say what'll ye gi' me wi' her?
Now, Woer, quo' he, I ha'e nae meikle,
But sick's I ha'e ye's get a Pickle,
With a fal, &c.

   A Kilnfu' of Corn I'll gi'e to thee,
Three Soums of Sheep, twa good Milk Ky,
Ye's ha'e the Wadding Dinner free,
   Troth I dow do na mair.
Content, quo' he, a Bargain be't,
I'm far frae hame, make hafte let's do't,
With a fal, &c.

   The Bridal Day it came to pass,
Wi' many a blythsome Lad and Lass;
But sicken a Day there never was,
   Sic Mirth was never seen.
This winsom Couple straked Hands,
Mess *John* ty'd up the Marriage Bands,
With a fal, &c.

              AND

And our Bride's Maidens were na few,
Wi' Tap-knots, Lug-knots a' in blew,
Frae Tap to Tae they were braw new,
   And blinked bonnilie.
Their Toys and Mutches were fae clean,
They glanced in our Ladfes Een,
With a fal, &c.

Sick Hirdum, Dirdum, and fick Din,
Wi' he o'er her and fhe o'er him,
The Minftrels they did never blin,
   Wi' meikle Mirth and Glee.
And ay they bobit and ay they berkt,
And ay their Wames together met,
With a fal, &c.

Z:

The promis'd Joy.

To the Tune of *Carle and the King come.*

WHen we meet again, Phely,
  When we meet again, Phely,
Raptures will reward our Pain,
And Loss result in Gain, Phely.

LONG the Sport of Fortune driv'n,
To Despair our Thoughts were giv'n,
But when Hell is turn'd to Heav'n,
  Our Odds will all be ev'n, Phely.
    When we meet again, Phely, &c.

Now in dreary distant Groves,
Tho we moan like Turtle-Doves,
Suffering best our Virtue proves,
  And will enhance our Loves, Phely,
    When we meet again, Phely, &c.

JOY

Joy will come in a Surprife,
'Till its happy Hour arife,
Temper well your love-fick Sighs,
  For Hope becomes the Wife, *Phely*.

    When we meet again, Phely,
    When we meet again Phely,
    Raptures will reward our Pain,
    And Lofs refults in Gain, Phely.

                      M.

To *DELIA on her drawing him to her Valantine.*

To the Tune of *Black Ey'd* Sufan.

YE Powers! was *Damon* then fo bleft
    To fall to charming *Delia's* Share,
Delia, the beauteous Maid, poffeft
  Of all that's foft and all that's fair?
Here ceafe thy Bounty, O indulgent Heav'n,
I afk no more, for all my Wifh is given.

                      J

I came, and *Delia* smiling show'd,
She smil'd and show'd the happy Name;
With rising Joy my Heart o'erflow'd,
I felt and blest the new born Flame.
May softest Pleasures ceaseless round her
    move,
May all her Nights be Joy, and Days be
    Love.

   She drew the Treasure from her Breast,
  That Breast where Love and Graces play,
  O Name beyond Expression blest!
  Thus lodg'd with all that's fair and gay.
To be so lodg'd! the Thought is Extasy,
Who would not wish in Paradise to ly?

                  R.

The

The faithful Shepherd.

To the Tune of *Auld lang fyne.*

WHEN Flow'ry Meadows deck the
    Year,
And fporting Lambkins play,
When fpangl'd Fields renewd appear,
    And Mufick wak'd the Day;
Then did my *Chloe* leave her Bower,
    To hear my am'rous Lay,
Warm'd by my Love, fhe vow'd no Power
    Shou'd lead her Heart aftray.

THE warbling Quires from ev'ry Bough
    Surround our Couch in Throngs,
And all their tuneful Art beftow,
    To give us Change of Songs;
Scenes of Delight my Soul poffeff'd,
    I blefs'd, then hug'd my Maid;
I rob'd the Kiffes from her Breaft,
    Sweet as a Noon-day's Shade.

JOY

Joy so transporting never fails
  To fly away as Air,
Another Swain with her prevails,
  To be as False as fair.
What can my fatal Passion cure?
  I'll never woo again,
All her Disdain I must endure,
  Adoring her in vain.

O.

What Pity 'tis to hear the Boy
  Thus sighing with his Pain;
But Time and Scorn may give him Joy
  To hear her sigh again.
Ah! fickle *Cloe*, be advis'd,
  Do not thy self beguile,
A faithful Lover should be priz'd,
  Then cure him with a Smile.

To

To Mrs. S. H. on her taking
something ill I said.

.To the Tune of *Hallow E'en*.

WHY hangs that Cloud upon thy
Brow?
That beauteous Heav'n ere while serene:
Whence do these Storms and Tempests flow,
Or what this Gust of Passion mean.
And must then Mankind lose that Light,
Which in thine Eyes was wont to shine,
And ly obscur'd in endless Night,
For each poor silly Speech of myne?

II

DEAR Child how can I wrong thy Name,
Since 'tis acknowledg'd at all Hands,
That could ill Tongues abuse thy Fame,
Thy Beauty can make large amends.
Or if I durst profanely try,
Thy Beauty's pow'rful Charms t'upbraid,
Thy Virtue well might give the Lie,
Nor call thy Beauty to its Aid.

For

For *Venus* every Heart t' enfnare,
With all her Charms has deckt thy Face,
And *Pallas* with unufual Care,
Bids Wifdom heighten every Grace.
Who can the double Pain endure?
Or who muft not refign the Field
To thee, Celeftial Maid, fecure
With *Cupid's* Bow and *Pallas'* Sheild?

If then to thee fuch Power is giv'n,
Let not a Wretch in Torment live,
But fmile and learn to copy Heav'n,
Since we muft fin ere it forgive.
Yet pitying Heaven not only does
Forgive th' Offender and th' Offence,
But even itfelf appeas'd beftows
As the Reward of Penitence.

H.

The Broom of Cowdenknows.

HOw blyth ilk Morn was I to fee
  The Swain come o'er the Hill ?
He skipt the Burn, and flew to me;
  I met him with good Will.
O the Broom, the bonny, bonny Broom,
  The Broom of Cowdenknows;
I wish I were with my dear Swain,
  With his Pipe and my Ewe.
I neither wanted Ew nor Lamb,
  While his Flock near me lay;
He gather'd in my Sheep at Night,
  And chear'd me a' the Day.
O the Broom, &c.
He tun'd his Pipe and Reed fae fweet,
  The Burds ftood liftning by;
Even the dull Cattle ftood and gaz'd,
  Charm'd with his Melody.
O the Broom, &c.

C

WHILE

WHILE thus we spent our Time by Turns,
  Betwixt our Flocks and Play;
I envy'd not the fairest Dame,
  Tho' ne'er sae rich and gay.
O the Broom, &c.

HARD Fate that I shou'd banish'd be,
  Gang heavily and mourn,
Because I lov'd the kindest Swain
  That ever yet was born.
O the Broom, &c.

HE did oblige me ev'ry Hour,
  Cou'd I but faithfu' be?
He flaw my Heart, cou'd I refuse
  What e'er he ask'd of me?
O the Broom, &c.

MY Doggie and my little Kit
  That held my wee Soup Whey,
My Plaidy, Broach and crooked Stick,
  May now ly useless by.

O the Broom, &c.

                  ADIEU

ADIEU, ye *Cowdenknows*, adieu,
　Farewel a' Pleasures there,
Ye Gods restore to me my Swain,
　Is a' I crave or care.
O the Broom, the bonny, bonny Broom,
　The Broom of Cowdenknows;
I wish I were with my dear Swain,
　With his Pipe and my Ewe.

S. R.

To CHLOE.

To the Time of, *I wish my Love were in
a Mire.*

O Lovely Maid! How dear's thy Pow'r?
　At once I love, at once adore;
With Wonder are my Thoughts possest,
While softest Love inspires my Breast.

C 2　　　　This

This tender Look, thefe Eyes of mine,
Confefs their am'rous Mafter thine;
Thefe Eyes with *Strephon*'s Paffion play,
Firft make me love and then betray.

Yes, charming Victor, I am thine,
Poor as it is, this Heart of mine
Was never in another's Pow'r,
Was never pierc'd by Love before.
In thee I've treafur'd up my Joy,
Thou can'ft give Blifs, or Blifs deftroy;
And thus I've bound myfelf to love,
While Blifs or Mifery can move.

O fhould I ne'er poffefs thy Charms,
Ne'er meet my Comfort in thy Arms,
Were Hopes of dear Enjoyment gone,
Still would I love, love thee alone.
But like fome difcontented Shade,
That wanders where its Body's laid,
Mournful I'd roam with hollow Glare,
For ever exil'd from my Fair.

L.

Upon hearing his Picture was in CHLOE's Breast.

To the Tune of *The Fourteen of* October.

YE Gods! was Strephon's Picture blest
With the fair Heaven of Chloe's Breast?
Move softer, thou fond fluttering Heart,
Oh gently throb, — too fierce thou art.
Tell me, thou brightest of thy Kind,
For Strephon was the bliss design'd?
For Strephon's Sake, dear charming Maid,
Didst thou prefer his wond'ring Shade?

AND thou blest Shade, that sweetly art
Lodg'd so near my Chloe's Heart,
For me the tender Hour improve,
And softly tell how dear I love.
Ungrateful Thing! it scorns to hear
Its wretched Master's ardent Pray'r,
Ingrossing all that beauteous Heaven,
That Chloe, lavish Maid, has given.

C 3.   I can.

I cannot blame thee ; were I Lord
Of all the Wealth thofe Breafts afford;
I'd be a Mifer too, nor give
An Alms to keep a God alive.
Oh fmile not thus, my lovely Fair;
On thefe cold Looks, that lifelefs Air,
Prize him whofe Bofom glows with Fire,
With eager Love and foft Defire.

'Tis true thy Charms, O powerful Maid,
To Life can bring the filent Shade;
Thou can'ft furpafs the Painter's Art,
And real Warmth and Flames impart,
But oh! it ne'er can love like me,
I've ever lov'd and lov'd but thee :
Then, Charmer, grant my fond Requeft,
Say thou canft love and make me bleft.

Song

Song for a Serenadè.

To the Tune of *The Broom of* Cowden knows.

TEACH me, *Chloe*, how to prove
My boasted Flame sincere;
'Tis hard to tell how dear I love,
And hard to hide my Care.

SLEEP in vain displays her Charms,
To bribe my Soul to Rest,
Vainly spreads her Silken Arms,
And courts me to her Breast.

WHERE can *Strephon* find Repose,
If *Chloe* is not there?
For ah! no Peace his Bosom knows,
When absent from the Fair.

WHAT tho *Phoebus* from on High
With-holds his chearful Ray;
Thine Eyes can well his Light supply,
And give me more than Day.

L.
Love

Love is the Cause of my Mourning.

BY a murmuring Stream a fair Shep-
herdeſs lay,

Be ſo kind, O ye Nymphs, I oftimes heard
her ſay,

Tell *Strephon*, I dy, if he paſſes this Way,

And that Love is the Cauſe of my mourning.

Falſe Shepherds that tell me of Beauty and
Charms,

You deceive me, for *Strephon's* cold Heart
never warms;

Yet bring me this *Strephon*, let me dy in
his Arms,

Oh Strephon the Cauſe of my mourning.

But firſt, ſaid ſhe, let me go

Down to the Shades below,

E'er ye let *Strephon* know,

That I have lov'd him ſo;

Then on my pale Cheek no Bluſhes will
ſhow

That Love was the Cauſe of my mourning.

Hæ

HER Eyes were scarce clofed when,
    Strephon came by,
He thought fhe'd been fleeping, and foft-
    ly drew nigh;
But finding her breathlefs, Oh Heavens,
    did he cry,
Ah Chloris *the Caufe of my mourning.*

Reftore me my *Chloris*, ye Nymphs ufe
    your Art,
They fighing, reply'd, 'Twas yourfelf
    fhot the Dart
That wounded the tender young Shep-
    herdefs Heart,
And kill'd the poor Chloris *with mourning.*

    Ah then is *Chloris* dead,
    Wounded by me! He faid,
    I'll follow thee, chafte Maid,
    Down to the filent Shade:
Then on her cold Snowy Breaft leaning
    his Head,
Expir'd the poor Strephon *with mourning.*
                X.

                    To

To Mrs. A. H. on seeing her at a Consort..

To the Tune of *The binniest Lass in a'-the Warld.*

Loox where my dear *Hamilla* smiles,
   Hamilla! heavenly Charmer,
See how with all their Arts and Wiles
   The *Loves* and *Graces* arm her.
A Blush dwells glowing on her Cheeks,
   Fair Seats of youthful Pleasures,
There Love in smiling Language speaks,
   There spreads his Rosy Treasures.

O fairest Maid, I own thy Pow'r,
   I gaze, I sigh and languish,
Yet ever, ever will adore,
   And triumph in my Anguish.
But ease, O Charmer, ease my Care,
   And let my Torments move thee;
As thou art fairest of the Fair,
   So I the dearest love thee.

                    2 C.

The bonny SCOT.

To the Tune of *The Boat-man*.

YE Gales that gently wave the Sea,
    And pleafe the canny Boat-man,
Bear me frae hence, or bring to me
  My brave, my bonny *Scot*—Man.
    In haly Bands
    We join'd our Hands,
  Yet may not this difcover,
    While Parents rate
    A large Eftate,
Before a faithfu' Lover.

BUT I loor chufe in *Highland* Glens
  To herd the Kid and Goat—Man,
E'er I cou'd for fic little Ends
  Refufe my bonny *Scot*—Man.

                Waq

Wae worth the Man
   Wha firſt began
The baſe ungenerous Faſhion,
   Frae greedy Views
   Love's Art to uſe,
While Strangers to its Paſſion.

FRAE foreign Fields, my lovely Youth,
   Haſte to thy longing Laſſie,
Wha pants to preſs thy bawmy Mouth,
   And in her Boſom hawſe thee.
     Love gi'es the Word,
     Then haſte on Board,
   Fair Winds and tenty Boat-man,
     Waft o'er, waft o'er
     Frae yonder Shore,
My blyth, my bonny Scot—Man.

Scornfu' Nansy.

To it's own Tune.

NANSY's to the *Green Wood* g'ne,
 To hear the *Gowdspink* chatring,
And *Willie* he has followed her,
 To gain her Love by flat'ring :
But a' that he cou'd say or do,
 She geck'd and scorned at him,
And ay when he began to woo,
 She bad him mind wha gat him.

WHAT ails ye at my Dad, quoth he,
 My Minny or my Aunty,
With Crowdy Mowdy they fed me,
 Lang-Kail and Ranty Taunty :
With Bannocks of good Barly Meal,
 Of thae there was right Plenty,
With chapped Stocks fou butter'd well,
 And was not that right dainty.

    D   ALTHO'

AL THO my Father was nae Laird,
  'Tis Daffin to be vaunty,
He keupit ay a good Kail-yard,
  A Ha' Houſe and a Pantrie:
A good blew Bonnet on his Head,
  An Owrlay 'bout his Cragy,
And ay untill the Day he died,
  He rade on good Shanks Nagy.

Now Wae and Wander on your Snour,
  Wad ye hae bony *Nanſy*,
Wad ye campare ye'r ſell to me,
  A Docken till a Tanſie?
I have a Wooer of my ain,
  They ca' him ſouple *Sandy*,
And well I wat his bony Mou
  Is ſweet like Sugar-Candy.

Wow *Nanſy*, What needs a' this Din?
  Do I not ken this *Sandy*?
I'm ſure the Chief of a' his Kin
  Was *Rab* the Beggar Randy;

His

His Minny Meg upo' her Back
 Bare baith him and his Billy;
Will ye compare a nasty Pack
 To me your winsome Willy?

Mr Gutcher left a good braid Sword,
 Tho it be auld and rusty,
Yet ye may tak it on my Word,
 It is baith stout and trusty;
And if I can but get it drawn,
 Which will be right uneasy,
I shall lay baith my Lugs in Pawn,
 That he shall get a Heezy.

Then *Nanfy* turn'd her round about,
 And said, did *Sandy* hear ye,
Ye wadna miss to get a Clout,
 I ken he disna fear ye:
Sae had ye'r Tonge and say nae mair,
 Set somewhere else your Fancy;
For as lang's *Sandy*'s to the fore
 Ye never shall get *Nanfy*. Z

Slighted Nanſy.

To the Tune of, *The Kirk wad let me be.*

'TIS I have ſeven braw new Gowns,
    And ither ſeven better to mak,
And yet for a' my new Gowns
    My Wooer has turn'd his Back.
Beſides I have ſeven Milk Ky,
    And *Sandy* he has but three ;
And yet for a' my good Ky,
    The Ladie winna ha'e me.

My Dady's a Delver of Dikes,
    My Mither can card and ſpin,
And I am a fine fodgel Laſs,
    And the Siller comes linkin in :
The Siller comes linkin in,
    And it is fou fair to ſee,
And fifty Times wow ! O wow !
    What ails the Lads at me ?

               WHEN

When e'er our Barn does bark,
Then fly to the Door I run;
To see gin ony young Spark
Will light and venture but in:
But never a ane will come in,
Tho' mony a ane gaes by,
Syne far ben the House I rin;
And a weary Wight am I.

WHEN I was at my first Pray'rs,
I pray'd but anes i' the Year,
I wish'd for a handsome young Lad,
And a Lad with muckle Gear.
When I was at my neist Pray'rs,
I pray'd but now and than,
I fash'd na my Head about Gear,
If I get a handsome young Man.

Now when I'm at my last Pray'rs,
I pray on baith Night and Day,
And O! if a Beggar wad come,
With that same Beggar I'd gae.

D 3   And

And O, And what'll come o' me?
And O, Whar'll I do?
That sic a braw Lassie as I
   Shou'd die for a Wooer I true !

Lucky Nanſy

To the Tune of, *Dainty Davy.*

WHILE Fops in saſt *Italian* Verſe,
   Ilk fair ane's Een and Breaſt rehearſe,
While Sangs abound and Scene is ſcarce,
   Theſe Lines I have indited :
But neither Darts nor Arrows here,
Venus nor *Cupid* ſhall appear,
And yet with theſe fine Sounds I ſwear,
   The Maidens are delited.

      I was ay telling you,
      Lucky Nanſy, *Lucky* Nanſy,
      Auld Springs wad ding the New,
      But ye wad never trow me.
                           NOR

Nor Snaw with Crimfon will I mix,
To fpread upon my Laffie's Cheeks,
And fyne th' unmeaning Name prefix,
  Mirinda, Chloe or *Phillis* :
I'll fetch nae Simile frae *Jove*,
My Height of Extafy to prove,
Nor fighing, ··· thus···prefent my Love,
  With Rofes eck and Lillies.
    I was ay telling you, &c.

But ftay, ··· I had amaift forgot
My Miftrefs and my Sang to Boot,
And that's an unko Faut I wate:
  But *Nanfy,* 'tis nae Matter.
Ye fee I clink my Verfe wi' Rhime,
And ken ye, that atones the Crime,
Forby, how fweet my Numbers chime,
  And flide awa like Water.
    I was ay telling you, &c.

Now

Now ken, my reverend sonsy Fair,
Thy runkled Cheek and lyart Hair,
Thy haff shut Een and hodling Air,—
    Are a' my Passion's Fewel.
Nae sky'ring Gowk, my Dear, can see
Or Love, or Grace, or Heaven in thee;
Yet thou haft Charms enew for me,
    Then smile and be na cruel.

> *Leeze me on thy Snawy Pow,*
> *Lucky Nansy, Lucky Nansy,*
> *Dryest Wood will eitkest low,*
> *And Nansy sae will ye now.*

TROTH I have sung the Sang to you,
Which ne'er anither Bard wad do;
Hear then my charitable Vow,
    Dear venerable *Nansy.*
But if the World my Passion wrang,
And say ye only live in Sang,
Ken I despise a slandring Tongue,
    And sing to please my Fancy.

> *Leeze me on thy. &c.*

Q.
A

A

Scots Cantata.

The Tune after an *Italian* Manner.

Compos'd by

Signior LORENZO BOCCHI.

RECITATIVE.

B LATE *Jonny* faintly teld fair *Jean* his
Mind,

Jeany took Pleasure to deny him lang

He thought her Scorn came frae a Heart
unkind,

Which gart him in Despair tune up this
Sang.

AIR.

O bony Laffie, since 'tis fae,
    That I'm despis'd by thee,
I hate to live; but O I'm wae,
    And unko sweet to die.

Dear

Dear Jeany, think what dowy Hours
   I thole by your Disdain;
Ah! should a Breast sae saft as yours
   Contain a Heart of Stane.

RECITATIVE.

THESE tender Notes did a' her Pity move,
With melting Heart she listned to the Boy;
O'ercome she smil'd, and promis'd him
       her Love:
He in Return thus sang his rising Joy.

AIR.

HENCE frae my Breast, contentious Care,
   Ye've tint the Power to pine,
My Jeany's good, my Jeany's fair,
   And a' her Sweets are mine.
O spread thine Arms and gi'e me Fowth
   Of dear enchanting Bliss,
A Thousand Joys around thy Mouth,
   Gi'e Heaven with ilka kiss.

The

The T O A S T.

To the Tune of, *Saw ye my* PEGGY.

COME let's ha'e mair Wine in,
  Bacchus hates Repining,
Venus loos na Dwining,
  Let's be blyth and free.
Away with dull here t' ye , Sir,
Ye'r Miftrefs .... gi'es her,
We'll drink her Health wi' Pleasure,
  Wha's belov'd by thee.

THEN let .... warm ye,
That's a Lafs can charm ye,
And to Joys alarm ye,
  Sweet is fhe to me.

                                    Some

Some Angel ye wad ca' her,
And never with ane brawer,
If ye bare-headed faw her,
  Kilter to the Knee.

.... a dainty Lass is,
Come let's join our Glasses,
And refresh our Haufes,
  With a Health to thee.
Let Coofs their Caih be clinking,
Be Statefmen tint in thinking,
While we with Love and Drinking,
  Give our Cares the Lie.

N. B.   *The firft Blank to be fupply'd with
the Toafter's Name, the two laft with
the Name of the Toaft.*

Maggie's Tocher.

To its ain Tune.

THE Meal was dear short syne,
We buckl'd us a' the gither;
And *Maggie* was in her Prime,
When *Willie* made Courtship till her,
Twa Pistals charg'd beguess,
To gie the courting Shot:
And syne came ben the Lass,
Wi' Swats drawn frae the Butt.
He first speer'd at the Guidman,
And syne at *Giles* the Mither,
An ye wad gi's a Bit Land,
We'e'd buckle us een the gither.

My Daughter ye shall hae,
I'll gi' you her by the Hand;
But I'll part wi' my Wife be my Tae,
Or I part wi' my Land.

E   Your

Your Tocher it fall be good,
There's nane fall hae its Maik,
The Lafs bound in her Snood,
And *Crummie* who kens her Stake;
With an auld Bedden o' Claiths,
Was left me be my Mither,
They're jet black o'er wi' Fleas,
Ye may cudle in them the gither.

   Ya fpeak right well, Guidman,
But ye maun mend your Hand,
And think o' Modefty,
Gin ye'll not quar your Land :
We are but young, ye ken,
And now we're gawn the gither.
A Houfe is butt and benn,
And *Crummie* will want her Fother.

The Pairns are coming on,
And they'll cry, O their Mither !
We hae nouther Pot nor Pan,
But four bare Legs the gither.

Your Tocher's be good enough,
For that ye need na fear,
Twa good Stilts to the Pleugh,
And ye your fell maun steer :
Ye shall hae twa good Pocks,
That anes were o' the Tweed,
The t'ane to had the Grots,
The ither to had the Meal.
With an auld Kist made o' Wands,
And that sall be your Coffer,
Wi' aiken Woody Bands,
And that may had your Tocher.

Consider well, Guidman,
We hae but borrow'd Gear,
The Horse that I ride on,
Is *Sandy Wilson's* Mare :
The Sadle's nane o' my ain,
An thae's but borrow'd Boots,
An whan that I gae hame
I maun tak to my Coots.

The

The Cloak is *Geordy Watt's*,
That gars me look fae croufe ;
Come fill us a Cogue of Swats,
We'll make na mair toom Rufe.

  I like you well, young Lad,
For telling me fae plain,
I married when little I had
O' Gear that was my ain.
But fin that Things are fae,
The Bride fhe maun come furth,
Tho a' the Gear fhe'll ha'e,
It'll be but little worth.
A Bargain it maun be,
Fy cry on *Giles* the Mither :
Content am I, quo' fhe,
E'en gar the Hiffie come hither.
The Bride fhe gade till her Bed,
The Bridegroom he came till her ;
The Fidler crap in at the Fit,
An they cudl'd it a the gither.

Z.

A

A SONG.

To the Tune of, *Blink over the Burn sweet* BETTIE.

LEAVE Kindred and Friends, sweet
    Betty,
  Leave Kindred and Friends, for me;
Assur'd, thy Servant is steddy
    To Love, to Honour, and Thee.
The Gifts of Nature and Fortune,
    May fly, by Chance, as they came;
They're Grounds the Destines sport on,
    But Virtue is ever the same.

ALTHO my Fancy were roving,
    Thy Charms so heavenly appear,
That other Beauties disproving,
    I'd worship thine only, my Dear.
And shou'd Life's Sorrows embitter
    The Pleasure we promis'd our Loves,
To share them, together, is fitter;
    Than moan, assunder, like Doves.

E 3   Out

Oh! were I but once so blessed,
    To grasp my Love in my Arms!
By thee to be grasp'd! and kissed!
    And live on thy Heaven of Charms!
I'd laugh at Fortune's Caprices,
    Shou'd Fortune capricious prove;
Tho Death shou'd tear me to Pieces,
    I'd die a Martyr to Love.   M.

A SONG.

To the Tune of, *The bonny Gray-ey'd Morning.*

CElestial Muses, tune your Lyres,
    Grace all my Raptures with your Lays,
Charming, enchanting *Kate* inspires,
In lofty Sounds her Beauties praise,
How undesigning she displays,
Such Scenes as ravish with Delight;
Tho brighter than Meridian Rays,
They dazle not, but please the Sight.
                              BLIND

BLIND God give this, this only Dart,
I neither will, nor can her harm,
I would but gently touch her Heart,
And try for once if that cou'd charm.
Go, *Venus*, use your fav'rite Wile,
As she is beauteous, make her kind,
Let all your Graces round her smile,
And sooth her till I Comfort find.

WHEN thus, by yielding, I'm o'erpaid,
And all my anxious Cares remov'd,
In moving Notes, I'll tell the Maid,
With what pure lasting Flames I lov'd.
Then shall alternate Life and Death,
My ravish'd flutt'ring Soul possess,
The softest tend'rest Things I'll breath,
Betwixt each am'rous fond Caress.

O,

SONG

SONG.

To the Tune of *the Broom of* Cowdenknows.

SUBJECTED to the Pow'r of Love,
   By *Nell's* refiftlefs Charms,
The Fancy fix'd no more can rove,
   Or fly Love's foft Alarms.
GAY *Damon* had the Skill to fhun
   All Traps by *Cupid* laid,
Until his Freedom was undone
   By *Nell* the conquering Maid.

BUT who can ftand the Force of Love,
   When fhe refolves to kill?
Her fparkling Eyes Love's Arrows prove,
   And wound us with our Will.

O happy *Damon*, happy Fair,
   What *Cupid* has begun,
May faithful *Hymen* take a Care
   To fee it fairly done.

G.

SONG.

SONG.

Tune of *Logan Water*.

Vitas hinnuleo me similis, Chloe.

TELL me, *Hamilla*, tell me why
   Thou doſt from him that loves thee
      run?
Why from his ſoft Embraces fly,
And all his kind Endearments ſhun?

So flies the *Fawn*, with Fear oppreſs'd,
Seeking its *Mother* ev'ry where,
It ſtarts at ev'ry empty Blaſt,
And trembles when no Danger's near.

AND yet I keep thee but in View,
To gaze the Glories of thy Face,
Not with a hateful Step purſue,
As Age to rifle every Grace.

CEASE then, dear Wildneſs, ceaſe to toy,
But haſte all Rivals to outſhine,
And grown mature, and ripe for Joy,
Leave *Mama*'s Arms and come to *mine*.
                  W.

A South-Sea Sang.

Tune of, *For our lang biding here.*

WHEN we came to *London* Town,
    We dream'd of Gowd in Gowp-
       ings here,
And rantinly ran up and down,
In rising Stocks to buy a Skair:
We daftly thought to row in Rowth,
But for our Daffine pay'd right dear;
The lave will fare the war in Trouth,
    For our lang biding here.

BUT when we find our Purses toom,
And dainty Stocks began to fa',
We hang our Lugs, and wi' a Gloom,
Girn'd at Stockjobbing ane and a'.
If ye gang near the *South-Sea* House,
The Whillywha's will grip ye'r Gear,
Syne a' the lave will fare the war,
    For our lang biding here.

Hap

Hap me with thy Petticoat.

O BELL thy Looks have kill'd my
   Heart,
I pafs the Day in Pain,
When Night returns I feel the Smart,
   And wifh for thee in vain.
I'm ftarving cold, while thou art warm,
   Have Pity and incline,
And grant me for a Hap that charm-
   ing Petticoat of thine.

My ravifh'd Fancy in Amaze,
   Still wanders o'er thy Charms,
Delufive Dreams ten thoufand Ways,
   Prefent thee to my Arms.
But waking think what I endure,
   While cruel you decline
Thofe Pleafures, which can only cure
   This panting Breaft of mine.

I

I faint, I fail, and wildly rove,
　　Becaufe you ftill deny
The juft Reward that's due to Love,
　　And let true Paffion die.
Oh! turn, and let Compaffion feife
　　That lovely Breaft of thine;
Thy Petticoat could give me Eafe,
　　If thou and it were mine.

SURE Heaven has fitted for Delight
　　That beauteous Form of thine,
And thou'rt too good its Law to flight,
　　By hindring the Defign.
May all the Powers of Love agree,
　　At length to make thee mine,
Or loofe my Chains, and fet me free
　　From ev'ry Charm of thine.

Love inviting Reason.

A SONG to the Tune of.—— *Chami me chatle, ne duce skar mi.*

WHEN innocent Paſtime our Pleaſure
    did crown,
Upon a green Meadow, or under a Tree,
E'er *Annie* became a fine Lady in Town,
How lovely and loving and bony was ſhe,
Rouze up thy Reaſon, my beautifu' *Annie*,
    Let ne'er a new Whim ding thy Fancy
    ajee,
O! as thou art bony be faithfu' and canny,
    And favour thy *Jamie* wha doats upon
    thee.

DOES the Death of a Lintwhite give *An-
    nie* the Spleen?
Can tyning of Trifles be uneaſy to thee?
Can Lap-dogs and Monkies draw Tears
    frae theſe Eeen,
    That look with Indifference on poor
    dying me?

P   Rouſe

Rouse up thy Reason, my beautifu' *Annie*,
 And dinna prefer a Paroquet to me,
O! as thou art bonny, be prudent and canny,
 And think on thy *Jamie*, wha doats u-
  pon thee.

Ah! shou'd a new Manto or *Flanders*
  Lace Head,
 Or yet a wee Cottie, tho never sae fine,
Gar thee grow forgetfu' and let his Heart
  bleed,
 That anes had some Hope of purchasing
  thine.
Rouse up thy Reason, my beautifu' *Annie*,
 And dinna prefer ye'r Fleegeries to me;
O! as thou art bony, be solid and canny,
 And tent a true Lover that doats upon
  thee.

Shall a *Paris* Edition of new fangle *Sany*,
 Tho gilt o'er wi' Laces and Fringes he be,
By adoring himself, be admir'd by fair
  Annie,
And aim at these Bennisons promis'd to me.
                    Rouse

Rouſe up thy Reaſon, my beautifu' *Annie*,
  And never prefer a light Dancer to me;
O! as thou art bony, be conſtant and canny,
  Love only thy *Jamie*, wha doats upon
    thee.

O! think, my dear Charmer, on ilka
  ſweet Hour,
  That ſlade away ſaftly between thee and
    me,
E'er Sqirrels or Beaus or Fopery had Power
  To rival my Love and impoſe upon thee.
Rouſe up thy Reaſon, my beautifu' *Annie*,
  And let thy Deſires be a' center'd in me,
O! as thou art bony, be faithfu' and canny,
  And love him wha's langing to center
    in the.

The Bob of Dunblane.

LAssie, lend me your braw Hemp
    Heckle,
And I'll lend you my Thripling Kame;
For Fainnefs, Deary, I'll gar ye keckle,
  If ye'll go dance the *Bob of Dunblane*.
Haft ye, gang to the Ground of ye'r
    Trunkies,
Busk ye braw and dinna think Shame;
Confider in Time, if leading of Monkies
  Be better than dancing the *Bob of Dun-*
    blane.

Be frank, my Laffie, left I grow fickle,
  And take my Word and Offer again,
Syne ye may chance to repent it mickle,
  Ye didna accept of the *Bob of Dunblane.*
The Dinner, the Piper and Prieft fhall be
    ready,
And I'm grown dowie with lying my lane,
Away then leave baith Minny and Dady,
  And try with me the *Bob of Dunblane.*

SONG

SONG *complaining of Ab-*
sence.

To the Tune of — *M's Apron, Deary.*

AH *Chloe!* thou Treasure, thou Joy
of my Breast,
Since I parted from thee I'm a Stranger
to Reft,
I fly to the Grove, there to languish and
and mourn,
There sigh for my Charmer, and long to
return.

The Fields all around me are smiling and
gay,
But they smile all in vain, — my *Chloe's* away;
The Field and the Grove can afford me no
Ease,—
But bring me my *Chloe* a Desart will please.

No Virgin I see that my Bosom alarms,
I'm cold to the fairest, tho' glowing with
Charms,
In vain they attack me, and sparkle the Eyes;
These are not the Looks of my *Chloe*, I cry.

These Looks where bright Love like the
    Sun sits enthron'd,
And smiling diffuses his Influence round,
'Twas thus I first view'd thee, my Char-
    mer, amaz'd;
Thus gaz'd thee with Wonder, and lov'd
    while I gaz'd.
   THEN, then the dear fair One was still
    in my Sight,
It was Pleasure all Day, it was Rapture
    all Night ;
But now, by hard Fortune remov'd from
    my Fair,
In Secret I languish, a Prey to Despair.
But Absence and Torment abate not my
    Flame,
My *Chloe*'s still charming, my Passion the
    same ;
Ol would the preserve me a Place in her
    Breast,
Then Absence would please me, for I
    would be blest.   R.

          SONG,

SONG.

To the Tune of, *I fixed my Fancy on her.*

BRIGHT *Cynthia's* Power divinely great,
  What Heart is not obeying?
A Thousand *Cupids* on her wait,
And in her Eyes are playing.
She seems the Queen of Love to reign;
For she alone dispences,
Such Sweets as best can entertain
The Gust of all the Senses.

HER Face a charming Prospect brings,
Her Breath gives balmy Blisses;
I hear an Angel when she sings,
And taste of Heaven in Kisses.
Four Senses thus she feasts with Joy,
From Nature's richest Treasure:
Let me the other Sense employ,
And I shall die with Pleasure.   **X.**

A

A SONG.

To the Tune of ...

TELL me, tell me, charming Creature,
  Will you never ease my Pain?
Must I die for every Feature?
  Must I always love in vain?
The Desire of Admiration,
  Is the Pleasure you pursue;
Pray thee try a lasting Passion,
  Such a Love as mine for you.

TEARS and sighing could not move you;
  For a Lover ought to dare:
When I plainly told I lov'd you,
  Then you said I went too far.
Are such giddy Ways beseeming,
  Will my Dear be fickle still?
Conquest is the Joy of Women,
  Let their Slaves be what they will.

                              YOUR

Your Neglect with Torment fill me,
  And my desperate Thoughts encrease;
Pray consider, if you kill me,
  You will have a Lover less.
If your wand'ring Heart is beating
  For new Lovers, let it be:
But when you have done coquetting,
  Name a Day and fix on me.

The REPLY.

IN vain, fond Youth, thy Tears give o'er;
  What more, alas! can *Flavia* do;
Thy Truth I own, thy Fate deplore:
  All are not happy that are true.
Suppress those Sighs, and weep no more;
  Should Heaven and Earth with thee
      combine,
'Twere all in vain, since any Power,
  To crown thy Love, must alter mine.
But if Revenge can ease thy Pain,
  I'll sooth the Ills I cannot cure,
Tell that I drag a hopeless Chain,
  And all that I inflict, endure.   X.

The

The Rose in YARROW.

To the Tune of *Mary Scot*.

'TWAS Summer and the Day was fair,
    Resolv'd a while to fly from Care,
Beguiling Thought, forgetting Sorrow,
I wander'd o'er the Braes of *Yarrow*;
Till then despising Beauty's Power,
I kept my Heart, my own secure :
But *Cupid's* Art did there deceive me,
And *Mary's* Charms do now enslave me.

WILL cruel Love no Bribe receive ?
No Ransom take for *Mary's* Slave ;
Her Frowns of Rest and Hope deprive me,
Her lovely Smiles like Light revive me.
No Bondage may with mine compare,
Since first I saw this charming Fair,
This beauteous Flower, the Rose of *Yarrow*,
In Nature's Gardens has no Marrow.

                       HAD

HAD I of Heaven but one Request,
I'd ask to ly in *Mary's* Breast;
There would I live or die with Pleasure,
Nor spare this World one Moment's Leisure,
Despising Kings, and all that's great,
I'd smile at Courts and Courtier's Fate;
My Joy complete on such a Marrow,
I'd dwell with her and live on *Yarrow*.

But tho' such Bliss I ne'er should gain,
Contented still I'll wear my Chain,
Inhopes my faithfull Heart may move her;
For leaving Life I'll always love her.
What Doubts distract a Lover's Mind?
That Breast all Softness must prove kind;
And she shall yet become my Marrow,
The lovely beauteous Rose of *Yarrow*.

C.

The

The Fair Penitent.

A SONG, — To its own Tune.

A Lovely Lass to a Friar came,
   To confess, in a Morning early,
In what, my Dear, are you to blame?
   Come own it all sincerely.
I've done, Sir, what I dare not name,
   With a Lad, who loves me dearly.

The greatest Fault in myself I know,
   Is what I now discover;
Then you to Rome for that must go,
   There Discipline to suffer.
Lake a Day Sir! if it must be so,
   Pray with me send my Lover.

No, no, my Dear, you do but dream,
   We'll have no double Dealing;
But if with me you'll repeat the same,
   I'll pardon your past failing.
I must own, Sir, tho' I blush for Shame,
   That your Penance is prevailing. X

The laſt *Time I came o'er the Moor.*

THE laſt Time I came o'er the Moor,
   I left my Love behind me;
Ye Pow'rs! What Pain do I endure
   When ſoft Ideas mind me?
Soon as the ruddy Morn diſplay'd
   The beaming Day enſuing,
I met betimes my lovely Maid,
   In fit Retreats for Wooing.

BENEATH the cooling Shade we lay,
   Gazing, and chaſtly ſporting;
We kiſs'd and promis'd Time away,
   'Till Night ſpread her black Curtain.
         G   1

I pitied all beneath the Skies,
  Ev'n Kings when she was nigh me;
In Raptures I beheld her Eyes,
  Which could but ill deny me.

Shou'd I be call'd where Cannons rore,
  Where mortal Steel may wound me;
Or cast upon some foreign Shore,
  Where Dangers may surround me:
Yet Hopes again to see my Love,
  To feast on glowing Kisses,
Shall make my Cares at Distance move,
  In Prospect of such Blesses.

In all my Soul, there's not one Place
  To let a Rival enter;
Since she excells in every Grace,
  In her my Love shall center.
Sooner the Seas shall cease to flow,
  Their Waves the *Alps* shall cover,
On *Greenland* Ice shall Roses grow,
  Before I cease to love her.

THE

THE next Time I go o'er the Moor,
  She shall a Lover find me;
And that my Faith it firm and pure,
  Tho' I left her behind me:
Then *Hymen's* sacred Bonds shall chain
  My Heart to her fair Bosom,
There, while my Being does remain,
  My Love more fresh shall blossom.

The Lass of Peatie's Mill.

THE Lass of *Peatie's* Mill,
  So bonny, blyth and gay,
In Spite of all my Skill,
Hath stole my Heart away.
When tedding of the Hay
Bare-headed on the Green,
Love 'midst her Locks did play,
And wanton'd in her Een.

HER

Her Arms white, round and smooth,
Breasts rising in their Dawn,
To Age it wou'd give Youth,
To prefs 'em with his Hand.
Thro' all my Spirits ran
An Extafy of Blifs,
When I fuch Sweetnefs find
Wrapt in a balmy Kifs.

WITHOUT the Help of Art,
Like Flowers which grace the Wild,
She did her Sweets impart,
When e'er fhe fpoke or fmil'd.
Her Looks they were fo mild,
Free from affected Pride,
She me to Love beguil'd,
I wifh'd her for my Bride.

O had I all that Wealth
Hoptoun's high Mountains fill,
Infur'd long Life and Health,
And Pleafures at my Will;

I'd

I'd promise and fulfill,
That none but bonny she,
The Lass of *Peatie*'s Mill
Shou'd share the same wi' me.

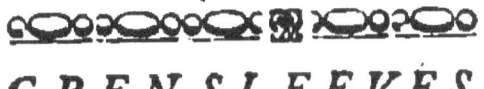

GRENSLEEVES.

YE watch'ul Guardians of the Fair,
    Who skiff on Wings of ambient Air,
Of my dear *Delia* take a Care,
    And represent her Lover
With all the Gayety of Youth,
With Honour, Justice, Love and Truth,
Till I return her Passions sooth,
    For me, in Whispers move her.

Be careful no base sordid Slave,
With Soul sunk in a golden Grave,
Who knows no Virtue but to save,
    With glaring Gold bewitch her.

G 3   Tell

Tell her for me she was defign'd,
For me who know how to be kind,
And have more Plenty in my Mind,
    Than one who's ten Times richer.

Let all the World turn upfide down,
And Fools run an eternal Round,
In Queft of what can ne'er be found,
    To pleafe their vain Ambition.
Let little Minds great Charms efpy
In Shadows which at Diftance ly,
Whofe hop'd for Pleafures, when come
      nigh,
    Prove nothing in Fruition.

But caft into a Mold Divine,
Fair *Delia* does with Luftre fhine,
Her virtuous Soul's an ample Mine,
    Which yields a conftant Treafure.
Let Poets in fublimeft Lays,
Imploy their Skill her Fame to raife;
Let Sons of Mufick pafs whole Days,
    With well-tun'd Reeds to pleafe her.

                          The

The *Yellow-hair'd Laddie.*

I N *April* when Primrofes paint the
    fweet Plain,
And Summer approaching rejoiceth the .
    Swain,
The *Yellow-hair'd Laddie* would often
    times go
To Wilds and deep Glens, where the
    Hawthorn-trees grow.

THERE under the Shade of an old Sa-
    cred Thorn,
With Freedom he fung his Loves Ev'ning
    and Morn;

H

He fang with fo faft and inchanting a
  Sound,

That *Silvans* and *Fairies* unfeen danc'd
  around.

THE Shepherd thus fang, Tho' young
  Maya be fair,

Her Beauty is dafh'd with a fcornfu' proud
  Air ;

But *Sufie* was handfome and fweetly could
  fing,

Her Breath like the Breezes perfum'd in
  the Spring.

THAT *Madie* in all the gay Bloom of
  her Youth,

Like the Moon was unconftant and never
  fpoke Truth ;

But *Sufie* was faithful, good humour'd and
  tree,

And fair as the Goddefs who fprung from
  the Sea.

THAT

THAT Mamma's fine Daughter, with
   all her great Dowr,
Was aukwardly airy, and frequently fowr:
Then, sighing, he wished, would Parents
   agree,
The witty sweet *Susie* his Mistress might be.

N A N N T O.

WHILE some for Pleasure pawn their
   Health,
 Twixt *Lais* and the *Bagnio*,
I'll save my self, and without Stealth
Kiss and caress my *Nanny-O*.
She bids more fair t'engage a *Jove*
Than *Leda* did or *Danae-O*,
Were I to paint the Queen of Love,
None else should sit but *Nanny-O*.

                   H o w

❀

How joyfully my Spirits rife,
When dancing fhe moves finely--O.
I guefs what Heav'n is by her Eyes,
Which fparkle fo divinely--O.
Attend my Vow, ye Gods, while I
Breath in the bleft *Britannia*,
None's Happinefs I fhall envy,
As long's ye grant me *Nanny*--O.

C H O R U S.

My bonny, bonny Nanny--O,
My lovely charming Nanny--O,
I care not though the World know
How dearly I love Nanny-O.

Bonny

Bonny JEAN.

LOVE's Goddess in a Myrtle Grove
Said, *Cupid*, bend thy Bow with speed,
Nor let the Shaft at Random rove,
For *Jeany's* haughty Heart must bleed.
The smiling Boy, with divine Art,
From *Paphos* shot an Arrow keen,
Which flew unerring to the Heart,
And kill'd the Pride of bonny *Jean*.

No more the Nymph, with haughty Air.
Refuses *Willie's* kind Address,
Her yielding Blushes shew no Care,
But too much Fondness to suppress.
No more the Youth is sullen now,
But lookes the gayest on the Green,
Whilst every Day he spies some new
Surprising Charms in bonny *Jean*.

A

A Thousand Transports crowd his
　　Breast,
He moves as light as fleeting Wind,
His former Sorrows seem a Jest,
Now when his *Jeanie* is turn'd kind;
Riches he looks on with Disdain,
The glorious Fields of War look mean;
The chearful Hound and Horn give Pain,
If absent from his bonny *Jean*.

THE Day he spends in am'rous Gaze,
Which even in Summer shorten'd seems,
When sunk in Downs with glad Amaze,
He wonders at her in his Dreams.
All Charms disclos'd, she looks more bright
Than *Troy's* Prize the *Spartan* Queen,
With breaking Day he lifts his Sight,
And pants to be with bonny *Jean*.

And

Throw the Wood Laddie.

O Sandy, why leaves thou thy *Nelly*
  to mourn?
  Thy Prefence cou'd eafe me,
  When naithing can pleafe me.
Now dowie I figh on the Bank of the
 Burn,
Or throw the Wood, Laddie, until thou
 return.

THo Woods now are bonny, and Mor-
 nings are clear,
  While Lav'rocks are finging,
  And Primrofes fpringing;
Yet nane of them pleafes my Eye or my
 Ear;
When throw the Wood Laddie ye dinna
 appear.

   H   THAT

THAT I am forsaken, some spare na
to tell;
  I'm fash'd wi' their Scorning,
  Baith Ev'ning and Morning;
Their Jeering gaes aft to my Heart wi' a
Knell;
When throw the Wood, Laddie, I wander
my sell.

THEN stay, my dear *Sandy*, nae lang-
er away,
  But quick as an Arrow,
  Haft here to thy Marrow,
Wha's living in Langour till that happy
Day;
When throw the Wood, Laddie, we'll
dance, sing, and play.

Down

Down the Burn Davie.

WHEN Trees did bud and Fields
    were green,
And Broom bloom'd fair to fee;
When *Mary* was complete fifteen,
    And Love laugh'd in her Eye,
Blyth *Davie*'s Blinks her Heart did move
    To fpeak her Mind thus free,
Gang down the Burn Davie, *Love,*
    And I fhall follow thee.

Now *Davie* did each Lad furpafs,
    That dwelt on this Burnfide,
And *Mary* was the bonnieft Lafs,
    Juft meet to be a Bride;

H 2   Her

Her Cheeks were rosie, red and white,
  Her Een were bonny blue;
Her Looks were like *Aurora* bright,
  Her Lips like dropping Dew.

As down the Burn they took their Way,
  What tender Tales they said;
His Cheek to hers he aft did lay,
  And with her Bosom play'd,
Till baith at length impatient grown,
  To be mair fully blest,
In yonder Vale they lean'd them down :
  Love only saw the rest.

What pass'd, I guess, was harmless Play,
  And naething sure unmeet;
For, ganging hame, I heard them say,
  They lik'd a Walk sae sweet;
And that they aften shou'd return
  Sic Pleasure to renew.
Quoth *Mary*, Love, I like the Burn,
  And ay shall follow you.

                          C.

SONG.

To the Tune of Gilder Roy.

AH! *Cloris*, cou'd I now but fit
   As unconcern'd, as when
Your Infant Beauty cou'd beget,
   No Happiness nor Pain.
When I this Dawning did admire,
   And prais'd the coming Day,
I little thought that rising Fire,
   Wou'd take my Rest away.

2.

Your Charms in harmless Child-hood lay,
   As Metals in a Mine.
Age from no Face takes more away,
   Than Youth conceal'd in thine:
But as your Charms insensibly
   To their Perfection prest;
So Love as unperceiv'd did fly,
   And center'd in my Breast.

H 3   Mr

My Paſſion with your Beauty grew,
   While *Cupid* at my Heart,
Still as his Mother favour'd you,
   Threw a new flaming Dart.
Each gloried in their wanton Part;
   To make a Lover, he
Employ'd the utmoſt of his Art—;
   To make a Beauty, ſhe.

                 X.

A SONG.

To the Tune of, *The yellow hair'd Laddie.*

YE Shepherds and Nymphs that a-
   dorn the gay Plain,
Approach from your Sports, and attend
   to my Strain;
Amongſt all your Number, a Lover ſo true,
Was ne'er ſo undone, with ſuch Bleſs in
   his View.

               WAS

WAs ever a Nymph so hard-hearted
 as mine ?
She knows me sincere, and she sees how I
 pine,
She does not disdain me, nor frown in her
 Wrath,
But calmly and mildly resigns me to Death.

 SHE calls me her Friend; but her Lover
  denies.
She smiles when I'm chearful, but hears
 not my Sighs:
A Bosom so flinty, so gentle an Air,
Inspires me with Hope, and yet bids me
 despair!

 I fall at her Feet, and implore her with
  Tears.
Her Answer confounds, while her Man-
 ner endears;
When softly she tells me to hope no Relief,
My trembling Lips bless her, in Spite of
 my Grief.

        By

. 1.

ny

nce

ea-

and

e ac-

like a

d her

cross

VEST

By Night while I flumber, ftill haunt-
ed with Care,

I ftart up in Anguifh, and figh for the Fair,

The Fair fleeps in Peace, may fhe ever do fo!

And only when dreaming imagine my Wo.

THEN gaze at a Diftance, nor farther
afpire,

Nor think fhe fhould love, whom fhe
cannot admire.

Hufh all thy Complaining, and dying her
Slave,

Commend her to Heaven, and thy felf to
the Grave.

By William Hamilton of Bargour.

SONG.

SONG.

To the Tune of, *When she came bye she bobbed.*

COME, fill me a Bumper, my jol'y
    brave Boys,
Lets have no more Female Impert'nence
    and Noise;
For I've try'd the Endearments and Plea-
    sures of Love,
And I find they're but Nonsense and
    Whimsies, by *Jove.*

WHEN first of all *Betty* and I were ac-
    quaint,
I whin'd like a Fool, and she sigh'd like a
    Saint:
But I found her *Religion,* her *Face* and her
    Love,
Were *Hypocrisy, Paint,* and *Self-interest,*
    by *Jove.*

SWEET

SWEET *Cecil* came next, with her languishing Air,
Her *Outside* was orderly, modest and fair,
But her *Soul* was sophisticate, so was her *Love*,
For I found she was only a *Strumpet*, by *Jove*.

LITTLE *double-gilt* Jenny's *Gold*
charm'd me at last;
(You know *Marriage and Money together*
does best)
But the *Baggage* forgetting her *Vows* and
her *Love*,
Gave her Gold to a *sniv'ling dull Coxcomb*,
by *Jove*.

COME fill me a Bumper then, jolly
brave Boys:
Here's a Farewell to Female Impert'nence
and Noise;
I know few of the Sex that are worthy my
Love;
And for *Strumpets* and *Jilts*, I abhor them,
by *Jove*.

L.
Dum-

Dumbarton's *Drums*.

DUMBARTON's Drums beat bonny O,
  When they mind me of my dear
        Jonny—O,
    How happy am I,
    When my Soldier is by,
While he kisses and blesses his *Annie*—O.
'Tis a Soldier alone can delight me—O;
For his graceful Looks do invite me—O:
    While guarded in his Arms,
    I'll fear no Wars Alarms,
Neither Danger nor Death shall e're fright
        me—O.

    My Love is a handsome Laddie—O;
Gentile, but ne're foppish nor gaudy—O;
    Tho' Commissions are dear,
    Yet I'll buy him one this Year;
For he shall serve no longer a Cadie—O,
                    A.

A Soldier has Honour and Bravery—O,
Unacquainted with Rogues and thei
  Knav'ry.—O;
    He minds no other Thing,
    But the Ladies or the King;
For every other Care is but Slavery—O·

Then I'll be the Captain's Lady—.O,
Farewell all my Friends, and my Daddy—·O,
    I'll wait no more at home,
    But I'll follow with the Drum,
And when e're that bears, I'll be ready—O.
Dumbarton's Drums found bonny···O,
They are sprightly like my Dear *Janny*···O,
    How happy shall I be,
    When on my Soldier's Knee,
And he kisses and blesses his *Annie*··O.
                            C.

Auld lang fyne.

SHOULD auld Acquaintance be forgot,
   Tho they return with Scars?
Thefe are the noble HERO's Lot,
   Obtain'd in glorious Wars:
Welcome, my VARO, to my Breaft,
   Thy Arms about me twine,
And make me once again as bleft,
   As I was lang fyne.

METHINKS around us on each Bough,
   A Thoufand *Cupids* play,
Whilft thro' the Groves I walk with you,
   Each Object makes me gay :
Since your Return the Sun and Moon
   With brighter Beams do fhine,
Streams murmure foft Notes while they run,
   As they did lang fyne.

        De-

Despise the Court and Din of State ;
   Let that to their Share fall,
Who can esteem such Slav'ry great,
   While bounded like a Ball ;
But sunk in Love, upon my Arms
   Let your brave Head recline,
We'll please our selves with mutual Charms,
   As we did lang syne.

O'er Moor and Dale, with your gay Friend,
   You may pursue the Chase,
And, after a blyth Bottle, end
   All Cares in my Embrace :
And in a vacant rainy Day
   You shall be wholly mine ;
We'll make the Hours run smooth away,
   And laugh at lang syne.

The Heroe pleas'd with the sweet Air
   And Signs of gen'rous Love,
Which had been utter'd by the Fair,
   Bow'd to the Pow'rs above ;

Next

Next Day with Confent and glad Hafte
Th' approach'd the facred Shrine,
Where the good Prieft the Couple bleft;
And put them out of Pine.

The Lafs of *Livingfton*.

Pain'd with her flighting James's Love,
    Bell dropt a Tear, — Bell dropt a
        Tear,
The Gods defcended from above,
    Well pleaf'd to hear,—Well pleaf'd to hear,
They heard the Praifes of the Youth
    From her own Tongue,——From her own
        Tongue,
Who now converted was to Truth,
    And thus fhe fung,——And thus fhe fung.

(100)

BLEST Days when our ingen'ous Sex,
More frank and kind,——More frank and
    kind,
Did not their lov'd Adorers vex,
But spoke their Mind, —— But spoke their
    Mind,
Repenting now she promis'd fair,
Wou'd he return,——Wou'd he return,
She ne'er again wou'd give him Care,
Or cause him mourn, —— Or cause him
    mourn.

WHY lov'd I the deserving **SWAIN**,
Yet still thought Shame, — Yet still
    thought Shame,
When he my yielding Heart did gain,
To own my Flame, — To own my Flame?
Why took I Pleasure to torment,
And seem too coy, — And seem too coy?
Which makes me now alas lament
My slighted Joy, — My slighted Joy.

             Y 2

Y e fair, while Beauty's in its Spring,
Own your Defire, -- Own your Defire,
While Love's young Power with his foft
    Wing
Fa'nq up the Fire, --- Fa'ns up the Fire-
O do not with a filly Pride, .
Or low Defign, -- Or low Defign,
Refufe to be a happy Bride,
But anfwer plain, -- But anfwer plain.

    T h u s the fair Mourner wail'd her
        Crime,
With flowing Eyes,--- With flowing Eyes,
Glad J a m i e heard her all the Time,
With fweet Surprife, -- With fweet
        Surprife. .
Some God had led him to the Grove,
His Mind unchang'd, -- His Mind un.
        chang'd ;
Flew to her Arms, and cry'd, My Love,
I am reveng'd ! -- I am reveng'd !
I 3   Peggy

Peggy, *I must love thee.*

AS from a Rock paft all Relief,
 The fhipwrackt COLIN fpying
His native Soil, o'ercome with Grief,
 Half funk in Waves and dying;
With the next Morning Sun he fpies
A Ship, which gives unhop'd Surprife,
New Life fprings up, he lifts his Eyes
 With Joy, and waits her Motion.

So when by her whom long I lov'd,
 I fcorn'd was and deferted,
Low with Defpair my Spirits mov'd,
 To be for ever parted :
Thus droopt I, till diviner Grace
I found in PEGGY's Mind and Face,
Ingratitude appear'd then bafe,
 But Virtue more engaging.

Then

THEN now since happily I've hit,
  I'll have no more delaying,
Let Beauty yield to manly Wit,
  We lose our selves in staying;
I'll haste dull Courtship to a Close,
Since Marriage can my Fears oppose,
Why should we happy Minutes lose,
  Since, *Peggy*, I must love thee?

MEN may be foolish if they please,
  And deem't a Lover's Duty,
To sigh, and sacrifice their Ease,
  Doating on a proud Beauty:
Such was my Case for many a Year,
Still Hope succeeding to my Fear,
False *Betty*'s Charms now disappear,
  Since *Peggy*'s far outshine them.

Betty

Beſſy Bell *and* Mary Gray.

O Beſſy Bell and Mary Gray,
   They are twa bonny Laſſes,
They bigg'd a Bower on yon Burn-brae,
And theek'd it o'er wi' Raſhes.
Fair Beſſy Bell I loo'd Yeſtreen,
And thought I ne'er cou'd alter;
But Mary Gray's twa pawky Een,
They gar my Fancy falter.

Now Beſſy's Hair's like a Lint Tap,
She ſmiles like a May Morning,
When Phœbus ſtarts ſrae Thetis' Lap,
The Hills with Rays adorning:
White is her Neck, ſaft is her Hand,
Her Waſte and Feet's ſow genty,
With ilka Grace ſhe can command,
Her Lips, O wow! they're dainty.

                                    And

AND *Mary's* Locks are like a Craw,
Her Eyes like Diamonds glances,
She's ay sa clean, redd-up and braw,
She kills when e'er she dances:
Blyth as a Kid, with Wit at Will,
She blooming tight and tall is;
And guides her Airs sae gracefu' still,
O *Jove!* she's like thy *Pallas.*

DEAR *Beſſy Bell* and *Mary Gray,*
Ye unco' fair oppreſs us:
Our Fancies jee between you twa,
Ye are sic bonny Laſſes:
Wae's me! for baith I canna get,
To ané by Law we're ſtented;
Then I'll draw Cuts, and take my Fate,
And be with ane contented.

T. II.

✤ ✤ ✤ ✤ ✤ ✤ ✤ ✤ ✤

I'll never leave thee.

JONNY.

THo' for seven Years and mair Honour thou'd reave me,
To Fields where Cannons raire, thou need
na grieve thee,
For deep in my Spirit thy Sweets are in-
dented,
And Love shall preserve ay what Love has
imprinted.
Leave thee, leave thee, I'll never leave thee,
Gang the Warld as it will, Dearest, believe
me.

NELLY.

O *Jonny*, I'm jealous when e'er ye discover
My Sentiments yielding, ye'll turn a loose
Rover ;

And

And nought i'the Warld wa'd rex my
    Heart fairer,

If you prove unconstant, and fancy an
    fairer :

Grieve me, grieve me, Oh it wad grieve me!

A'the lang Night and Day, if you deceive
    me.

JONNY.

MY Nelly, let never sic Fancies oppress ye,

For while my Blood's warm I'll kindly
    caress ye;

Your blooming saft Beauties first beeted
    Love's Fire,

Your Virtue and Wit make it ay flame
    the higher.

Leave thee, leave thee, I'll never leave thee,

Gang the Warld as it will, Dearest, be-
    lieve me.

NELLY.

TRUE, Jonny, I frankly this Minute
    allow ye

To think me your Mistress, for Love gars
    me trew ye,   And

And gin ye prove fa'fe, to ye'r fell be it
said then,

Ye'll win but sma' Honour to wrang a
kind Maiden :

Reave me, reave me, Heavens! It wad
reave me

Of my Reft Night and Day, if ye deceive
me.

JONNY.

BID Iceshogles hammer red Gauds on
the Studdy,

And fair Simmer Mornings nae mair appear ruddy,

Bid *Britons* think ae Gate, and when they
obey ye,

But never till that Time, believe I'll betray ye :

Leave thee, leave thee, I'll never leave thee;

The Starns shall gang withershins e'er I
deceive thee.

THE

My Deary, if thou die.

LOVE never more shall give me Pain,
  My Fancy's fix'd on thee;
Nor ever Maid my Heart shall gain,
  My Peggy, if thou die.
Thy Beauties did such Pleasure give,
  Thy Lov's so true to me:
Without thee I shall never live,
  My Deary, if thou die.

If Fate shall tear thee from my Breast,
  How shall I lonely stray?
In dreary Dreams the Night I'll waste,
  In Sighs the silent Day.
I ne'er can so much Virtue find,
  Nor such Perfection see;
Then I'll renounce all Woman-kind,
  My Peggy, after thee.

K   No

No new blown Beauty fires my Heart,
   With *Cupid*'s raving Rage,
But thine which can such Sweets impart,
   Must all the World engage.
'Twas this that like the Morning-Sun
   Gave Joy and Life to me,
And when its destin'd Day is done,
   With *Peggy* let me die.

Ye Powers that smile on virtuous Love,
   And in such Pleasure share;
You who its faithful Flames approve,
   With Pity view the Fair.
Restore my *Peggy*'s wonted Charms,
   Those Charms so dear to me:
Oh! never rob them from those Arms;
   I'm lost, if *Peggy* die.

                                 C.

                                 My

My Jo Janet.

SWEET Sir, for your Courtesse,
　　When ye came by the *Bass* then.
For the Love ye bear to me,
　　Buy me a Keeking-glass then.
Keek into the Draw-well
　　　　Janet, Janet,
And there ye'll see ye'r bonny sell,
　　　My Jo Janet.

KEEKING in the Draw-well clear
　　What if I shou'd fa' in,
Syn a' my Kin will say and swear
　　I drown'd my sell for Sin.
Ha'd the better be the Brae,
　　　　Janet, Janet,
Ha'd she better be the Brae,
　　　My Jo Janet.

K 2　　　　　　　GOOD

※

Good·Sir, for your Courtesie,
  Coming through *Aberdeen* then,
For the Love ye bear to me
  Buy me a Pair of Shoon then.
Clout the auld, the new are dear,
    Janet, Janet;
At Pair may gain ye haff a Year,
    My Jo Janet.

※

But what if dancing on the Green,
  And skipping like a Mawking,
If they shou'd see my clouted Shoon,
  Of me they will be mauking.
Dance ay laigh and late as E'en,
    Janet, Janet;
Syne a' their Fauts will no be seen,
    My Jo Janet.

KIND

KIND Sir, for your Courtesie,
  When ye gae to the Cross then,
For the Love ye bear to me,
  Buy me a pacing Horse then.
Pace upo' your Spinning-wheel,
      Janet, Janet;
Pace upo' your Spinning-wheel,
      My Jo Janet.

MY Spinning-wheel is auld and stiff,
  The Rock o't winna stand, Sir,
To keep the Temper-pin in tiff
  Employs aft my Hand, Sir ;
Make the best o't that ye can,
      Janet, Janet;
But like it never wale a Man,
      My Jo Janet.

SONG

SONG.

To the Tune of, John Anderſon my Jo.

WHAT means this Niceneſs now of late,
    Since Time that Truth does prove;
Such Diſtance may conſiſt with State,
    But never will with Love.
'Tis either Cunning or Diſdain
    That does ſuch Ways allow;
The firſt is baſe, the laſt is vain:
    May neither happen you.

For if it be to draw me on,
    You over-act your Part;
And if it be to have me gone,
    You need not haff that Art:
For if you chance a Look to caſt,
    That ſeems to be a Frown,
I'll give you all the Love that's paſt,
    The reſt ſhall be my own.

               Anſd

Auld Rob Moris.

MITHER.

AULD *Rob Moris* that wins in yon Glen,
He's the King of good Fellows, and
Wale of auld Men,
Has fourscore of black Sheep, and four-
score too;
Auld *Rob Moris* is the Man ye maun loo.

DOUGHTER.

Ha'd your Tongue Mither, and let that abee;
For his Eild and my Eild can never agree:
They'll never agree, and that will be seen;
For he is Fourscore, and I'm but Fifteen.

MITHER.

Ha'd your Tongue, Doughter, and lay
by your Pride,
For he's be the Bridegroom, and ye's be
the Bride;
He shall ly by your Side, and kiss ye too,
Auld *Rob Moris* is the Man ye maun loo.

DOUGH.

DOUGHTER.

AULD *Rob Moris* I ken him fou weel,
His A---- it sticks out like ony Peet-Creel,
He's out-shin'd, in-kneed and ringle-eyd too;
Auld *Rob Moris* is the Man I'll ne'er loe.

MITHER.

THO' auld *Rob Moris* be an elderly Man,
Yet his auld Brass it will buy a new Pan;
Then, Doughter, ye shoudna be sae ill to
    shoo,
For auld *Rob Moris* is the Man ye maun
    loo.

DOUGHTER.

BUT auld *Rob Moris* I never will hae,
His Back is sae stiff, and his Beard is grown
    gray;
I had titter die than live wi' him a Year;
Sae mair of *Rob Moris* I never will bear.
                   Q.

SONG.

SONG.

To the Tune of, Come kiss with me, come clap with me, *&c.*

PEGGY.

MY *Jocky* blyth for what thou haſt
    done,
  There is nae help nor mending;
For thou haſt jog'd me out of Tune,
  For a' thy fair pretending.
My Mither ſees a Change on me,
  For my Complexion daſhes,
And this, alas! has been with thee
  Sae late amang the Raſhes.

                   JOCKY.

JOCKY.

My *Peggy*, what I've faid I'll do,
 To free thee frae her Scouling;
Come then and let us buckle to,
 Nae langer let's be fooling :
For her Content I'll inftant wed,
 Since thy Complexion dafhes;
And then we'll try a Feather-bed,
 'Tis fafter than the Rafhes.

PEGGY.

THEN *Jocky* fince thy Lov's fae true,
 Let Mither fcoul, I'm eafy:
Sae langs I live I ne'r fhall rue
 For what I've done to pleafe thee,
And there's my Hand I's ne'er complain.
 O! wells me on the Rafhes;
When e'er thou likes I'll do't again,
 And a Feg for a' their Clafhes.

Z.

SONG.

SONG.

To the Tune of Rothes's Lament; *or,* Pinky-House.

A S *Silvia* in a Forreſt lay
  To vent her Woe alone;
Her Swain *Sylvander* came that Way,
 And heard her dying Moan.
Ah! is my Love (ſhe ſaid) to you
 So worthleſs and ſo vain :
Why is your wonted Fondneſs now
 Converted to Diſdain ?

You vow'd the Light ſhou'd Darkneſs turn
 E'er you'd exchange your Love;
In Shades now may Creation mourn,
 Since you unfaithful prove.
Was it for this I Credit gave
 To every Oath you ſwore ?
But ah! it ſeems they moſt deceive
 Who moſt our Charms adore.

       Tis

'TIs plain your Dift was all Deceit,
  The Practice of Mankind:
Alas! I see it but too late,
  My Love hath made me blind.
For you, delighted I could die:
  But Oh! with Grief I'm fill'd
To think that credulous conftant I
  Should by your felf be kill'd.

THIS faid, —all breathlefs, fick and pale,
  Her Head upon her Hand,
She found her vital Spirits fail,
  And Senfes at a Stand.
Sylvander then began to melt:
  But e're the Word was given
The heavy Hand of Death fhe felt,
  And figh'd her Soul to Heaven.

                                    M.

                                   The

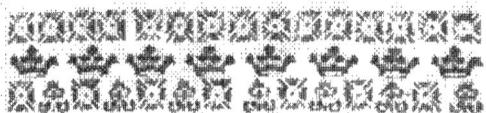

The *Young* Laird *and* Edinburgh Katy.

NOw wat ye wha I met Yeſtreen,
  Coming down the Street, my Jo,
My Miſtreſs in her Tartan Screen,
Fow bonny, braw aud ſweet, my Jo?
My Dear, quoth I, Thanks to the Night
That never wiſht a Lover ill,
Since ye're out of your Mither's Sight,
Let's take a Wauk up to the Hill.

O Katty, wiltu gang wi' me,
And leave the dinſome Town a while,
The Bloſſom's ſprouting frae the Tree,
And a' the Summer's gawn to ſmile;

L   The

The Mavis, Nightingale and Lark,
The bleating Lambs and whistling Hynd,
In ilka Dale, Green, Shaw and Park,
Will nourish Health and glad y'er Mind.

Soon as the clear Goodman of Day
Bends his Morning Draught of Dew,
We'll gae to some Burnside and play,
And gather Flowers to busk ye'r Brow,
We'll pou the Daisies on the Green,
The lucken Gowans frae the Bog;
Between Hands now 'and then we'll lean,
And sport upo' the Velvet Fog.

There's up into a pleasant Glen,
A wee Piece frae my Father's Tower,
A canny, saft and flowry Den,
Which circling Birks have form'd a Bower:
When e'er the Sun grows high and warm,
We'll to the cauller Shade remove,
There will I lock thee in mine Arm,
And love and kiss, and kiss and love.

KATY's

KATY's *Answer.*

MY Mither's ay glowran o'er me,
Tho' she did the same before me,
    I canna get Leave,
        To look to my Loove,
Or else she'll be like to devour me.

RIGHT fain wad I take ye'r Offer,
Sweet Sir, but I'll tine my Tocher,,
    Then, *Sandy,* yell frer,
        And wyte y'er poor *Katt,*
When e'er ye keek in your toom Coffer.

FOR tho' my Father has Plenty
Of Siller and Plenish ng da'nty,
    Yet he's unco sweer
        To twin wi' his Gear,
And sae we had need to be tenty.

TUTOR my Parents wi' Caution,
Be wylie in Ilka Motion,
    Brag well o' ye'r Land,
        And there's my leal Hand,
Win them, I'll be at your Devotion.

L 3   *MARY*

MARY SCOT.

HAPPY's the Love which meets Return,
When in soft Flames Souls equal burn;
But Words are wanting to discover
The Torments of a hopeless Lover.
Ye Registers of Heav'n, relate,
If looking o'er the Rolls of Fate,
Did you there see me mark'd to marrow,
Mary Scot, the Flower of *Yarrow.*

II.

An no! her Form's too heavenly fair,
Her Love the Gods above must share,
While Mortals with Despair explore her,
And at a Distance due adore her.
O lovely Maid, my Doubts beguile!
Revive and bless me with a Smile,
Alas if not, you'll soon debar a
Sighing Swain the Banks of *Yarrow.*

B 2

Be huſh, ye Fears, I'll not deſpair,
My *Mary's* tender as ſhe's fair;
Then I'll go tell her all mine Anguiſh,
She is too good to let me languiſh;
With Succeſs crown'd, I'll not envy
The Folks who dwell above the Sky,
When *Mary Scot's* become my Marrow,
We'll make a Paradice on *Yarrow*.

O'er BOGIE.

I Will awa' wi' my *Love*,
  I will awa' wi' her,
Tho' a' my *Kin* had ſworn and ſaid,
  I'll o'er Bogie *wi' her.*

If I can get but her Conſent,
  I dinna care a Strae,
Tho ilka ane be diſcontent,
  Awa' wi' her I'll gae.
I will awa', &c.

L 3   Fog

For now she's Mistress of my Heart,
  And wordy of my Hand,
And well I wat we shanna' part
  For Siller or for Land.
Let Rakes delyte to swear and drink,
  And Beaus admire fine Lace,
But my chief Pleasure is to blink
  On *Betty's* bonny Face.
I will awa' &c.

There a' the Beauties do combine,
  Of Colour, Treats and Air,
The Saul that sparkles in her Een
  Makes her a Jewel rare ;
Her flowing Wit gives shining Life
  To a' her other Charms,
How blest I'll be when she's my Wife,
  And lockt up in my Arms.
I will awa', &c.

There blythly will I rant and sing,
  While o'er her Sweets I range,
I'll cry, Your humble Servant, King,
  Shame fa' them that wa'd change :

A

A Kiſs of *Betty* and 'a Smile,
 Abeet ye wad lay down,
The Right ye ha'e to *Britain*'s Iſle,
 And offer me ye'r Crown.
I will awa', &c.

O'er the Moor to M A G G Y.

A N D I'll o'er the Moor to *Maggy*,
 Her Wit and Swe-tneſs call me,
Then to my Fair I'll ſhow my Mind,
 Whatever may befall me.
If ſhe love Mirth, I'll learn to ſing,
 Or likes the Nine to follow.
I'll lay my Lugs in *Pindus* Spring,
 And invocate *Apollo*,

IF she admire a martial Mind,
   I'll sheath my Limbs in Armour;
If to the softer Dance inclin'd,
   With gayest Airs I'll charm her;
If she love Grandeur, Day and Night
   I'll plot my Nation's Glory,
Find Favour in my Prince's Sight,
   And shine in future Story.

BEAUTY can Wonders work with Ease,
   Where Wit is corresponding,
And bravest Men know best to please,
   With Complaisance abounding.
My bonny *Maggy*'s Love can turn
   Me to what Shape she pleases,
If in her Breast that Flame shall burn,
   Which in my Bosom blazes.

Pol-

Polwart *on the* GREEN.

AT Polwart *on the Green*
If you'll meet me the Morn, .
Where Lasses do conveen
To dance about the Thorn, .
A kindly Welcome you shall meet
  Frae her wha likes to view
A Lover and a Lad compleat,
  The Lad and Lover you.

LET dorty Dames say *Na,*
As lang as e'er they pleafe,
Seem caulder than the Sna',
While inwardly they bleez;
But I will frankly shaw my Mind,
  And yield my Heart to thee;
Be ever to the Captive kind,
  That langs na to be free.

A T

At *Polwart on the Green*,
Amang the new mawn Hay,
With Sangs and Dancing keen
We'll pals the heartfome Day.
As Night if Beds be o'er thrang laid,
* And thou be twin'd of thine,*
Thou shalt be welcome, my dear Lad,
* To take a Part of mine.*

John Hay's *Bonny Lassie.*

BY fmooth winding *Tay* a Swain was
     reclining,
Aft cry'd he, Oh hey! Maun I ftill live
     pining
My fell thus away, and darna difcover
To my bonny *Hay* that I am her Lover?

NA

Nae mair it will hide, the Flame waxes
    stranger,
If she's not my Bride, my Days are nae
    langer;
Then I'll take a Heart, and try at a Ven-
    ture,
May be, e'er we part, my Vows may con-
    tent her.

She's fresh as the Spring, and sweet as
    Aurora,
When Birds mount and sing, bidding Day
    a Good-morrow.
The Sward of the Mead, enamel'd with
    Daisies,
Look wither'd and dead, when twin'd of
    her Graces.

But if she appear, where Verdures in-
    vite her,
The Fountains run clear, and Flowers
    smell the sweeter :

To

'Tis Heaven to be by, when her Wit is a
   flowing,

Her Smiles and bright Eye set my Spirits
   a glowing.

The mair that I gaze, the deeper I'm
   wounded,

Struck dumb with Amaze, my Mind is
   confounded:

I'm all in a Fire, dear Maid, to caress ye,

For a' my Desire is *HAY*'s bonny Lassie.

Katha-

Katharine Ogie.

AS walking forth to view the Plain,
   Upon a Morning early,
While *May's* sweet Scent did chear my
    Brain,
   From Flowers which grow so rarely;
I chanc'd to meet a pretty Maid,
   She shin'd tho' it was fogie:
I ask'd her Name; sweet Sir, she said,
   My Name is *Katharine Ogie*.

I stood a while, and did admire,
   To see a Nymph so stately;
So brisk an Air there did appear
   In a Country-Maid so neatly;

       M   Such

Such natural Sweetness she display'd,
  Like a Lillie in a Bogie ;
Diana's self was ne'er array'd
  Like this same *Katharine Ogie*.

Thou Flower of Femals, Beauty's Queen,
  Who sees thee sure must prize thee ;
Tho' thou art drest in Robes but mean,
  Yet these cannot disguise thee ;
Thy handsome Air, and graceful Look
  Far excells any clownish Rogie ;
Thou'rt Match for Laird, or Lord or Duke,
  My charming *Katharine Ogie*.

O were I but some Shepherd-Swain,
  To feed my Flock beside thee,
At Boughting-time to leave the Plain,
  In milking to abide thee,
I'd think my self a hapier Man,
  With *Kate*, my Club, and Dogie,
Than he that hugs his Thousands ten,
  Had I but *Katharine Ogie*.

THE

THEN I'd defpife the Imperial Throne
  And Statefmen's dangerous Stations;
I'd be no King, I'd wear no Crown,
  I'd fmile at conquering Nations;
Might I carrefs, and ftill poffefs,
  This Lafs of whom I'm vogie;
For thefe are Toys, and ftill look lefs,
  Compar'd with *Katharine Ogie*.

BUT I fear the Gods have not decree'd
  For me fo fine a Creature,
Whofe Beauty rare makes her exceed
  All other Works in Nature.
Clouds of Defpair furround my Love,
  That are both dark and fogie.
Pity my Cafe, ye Powers above,
  Elfe I die for *Katharine Ogie*.

X.

M 2   An

Ann thou were my ain Thing.

OF Race divine thou needs muſt be,
   Since nothing earthly equals thee;
For Heaven's Sake, Oh! favour me,
  Who only lives to love thee.

> *Ann thou were my ain Thing,*
> *I would love thee, I would love thee,*
> *Ann thou were my ain Thing,*
> *How dearly would I love thee!*

THE Gods one Thing peculiar have,
To mine none whom they can ſave;
O! for their Sake ſupport a Slave,
  Who only lives to love thee.

> *Ann thou were, &c.*

                  To

To Merit I no Claim can make,
But that I love, and for your Sake,
What Man can name, I'll undertake,
   So dearly do I love thee.
    Ann thou were, &c.

My Paſſion, conſtant as the Sun,
Flames ſtronger ſtill, will ne'er have done
Till Fates my Threed of Life have ſpun,
   Which breathing out, I'll love thee.
    Ann thou were, &c.

                  X.

Like Bees that ſuck the Morning Dew,
Frae Flowers of ſweeteſt Scent and Hew,
Sae wad I dwell upo' thy Mou,
   And gar the Gods envy me.
    Ann thou were, &c.

       Sae

Sae lang's I had the Use of Light,
I'd on thy Beauties feast my Sight,
Syn in saft Whispers through the Night,
   I'd tell how much I lo'd thee.
     Ann thou wert, &c.

How fair and ruddy is my *Jean*,
She moves a Goddess o'er the Green :
Were I a King, thou shou'd be Queen,
   Nane but my sell aboon thee.
     Ann thou were, &c.

I'd grasp thee to this Breast of mine,
Whilst thou, like Ivy or the Vine,
Arround my stronger Limbs shou'd twine,
   Form'd hardy to defend thee.
     Ann thou were, &c.

Time's on the Wing, and will not stay,
In shining Youth, let's make our Hay,
Sinte Love admits of nae Delay,
   O let nae Scorn undo thee.
     Ann thou wert, &c.

WHILE

WHILE Love does at his Altar ſtand,
Hae there's my Heart, gi'e me thy Hand,
And, with ilk Smile, thou ſhalt command
   The Will of him wha loves thee.
     Ann thou were, &c.

There's my Thumb I'll ne'er beguile thee.

MY ſweeteſt *May,* let Love incline thee
   T' accept a Heart which he de-
    ſigns thee;
And, as your conſtant Slave, regard it,
Syne for its Faithfulneſs reward it;
'Tis Proof-a-ſhot to Birth or Money,
But yields to what is ſweet and bonny;
Receive it then with a Kiſs and a Smily,
There's my Thumb it will ne'er beguile ye.
                 How

How tempting sweet thefe Lips of thine
    are,
Thy Bofom white, and Legs fa fine are,
That when in Pools I fee thee clean 'em,
They carry away my Heart between 'em ;
I wifh, and I wifh, while it gaes duntin,
O gin I had thee on a Mountain,
Tho' Kith and Kin and a' fhou'd revile thee,
There's my Thumb I'll ne'er beguile thee.

ALANE through flow'ry Hows I dander,
Tenting my Flocks, left they fhou'd wander,
Gin thou'll gae alang, I'll dawt thee gaylie,
And gi'e my Thumb I'll ne'er beguile thee.
O my dear Laffie, it is but Daffin
To had thy Woer up ay niff naffin.
That Na, na, na, I hate it moft vilely,
O fay, Yes, and I'll ne'er beguile thee.

For

For the Love of J E A N.

JOCKY faid to Jeany, Jeany, wilt thou
     do't ?
Ne'er a fit, quo' Jeany, for my Tochergood,
For my Tochergood I winna marry
    thee.
Eens ye like, quo' Jonny, ye may let it be.

I ha' Gowd and Gear, I ha' Land enough,
I ha' feven good Owfen ganging in a
    Pleugh,
Ganging in a Pleugh, and linking o'er the
    Lee;
And gin ye winna take me, I can let ye be.

I

I ha'a good Ha'Houſe, a Barn and a Byer,
A Stack afore the Door, I'll make a rantin
    Fire;
I'll make a rantin Fire, and merry ſhall
    we be;
And gin ye winna take me, I can let ye be.

Jeaſy ſaid to Jocky, gin ye winna tell,
Ye ſhall be the Lad, I'll be the Laſs my
    ſell;
Ye're a bonny Lad, and I'm a Laſſie free,
Ye're welcomer to tak me, than to let
    me be.

                   Z.

S O N G.

SONG.

To the Tune of, PEGGY, *I muſt love thee.*

BENEATH a Beech's grateful Shade,
   Young *Colin* lay complaining;
He ſigh'd, and ſeem'd to love a Maid,
   Without Hopes of obtaining;
For thus the Swain indulg'd his Grief,
   Tho' Pity cannot move thee,
Tho' thy hard Heart gives no Relief,
   Yet, *Peggy,* I muſt love thee.

SAY, *Peggy,* what has *Colin* done,
   That thus you cruelly uſe him?
If Love's a Fault, 'tis that alone,
   For which you ſhould excuſe him:

Twas

'Twas thy dear self first rais'd this Flame,
 · This Fire by which I languish;
'Tis thou alone can quench the same,
 And cool its scorching Anguish.

II

For thee I leave the sportive Plain,
 Where every Maid invites me;
For thee, sole Cause of all my Pain,
 For thee that only slights me;
This Love that fires my faithful Heart
 By all but thee's commended.
Oh! wouldst thou act so good a Part,
 My Grief might soon be ended.

III

That beauteous Breast so soft to feel,
 Seem'd Tenderness all over,
Yet it defends thy Heart like Steel,
 'Gainst thy despairing Lover.
Alas! tho' it should ne'er relent,
 Nor Colin's Care e're move thee,
Yet till Life's latest Breath is spent,
 My Peggy, I must love thee.

C

Genty TIBBY, *and sonsy* NELLY.

To the Tune of Tibby Fowler in the Glen.

TIBBY has a Store of Charms,
  Her genty Shape our Fancy warms,
How strangely can her sma white Arms
  Ferrer the Lad, wha looks but at her?
Frae 'er Ancle to her slender Waste,
  These Sweets conceal'd invite to dawt
      her,
Her rosie Cheek and rising Breast,
  Gar ane's Mouth gush bowt fou' o' Wa.
    ter.

NELLY's gawsy, saft and gay,
Fresh as the lucken Flowers in May,
Ilk ane that sees her, cries Ah hey!
  She's bonny, O I wonder at her!
        N   The

The Dimples of her Chin and Cheek,
   And Limbs fae plump, invite to daw ther,
Her Lips fae fweet, and Skin fae fleek,
   Gar mony Mouths befide mine water.

Now ftrike my Finger in a Bore,
My Wyfon with the Maiden fhore,
Gin I can tell whilk I am for,
   When thefe twa Stars appear thegither.
O Love! why doft thou gi'e thy Fires
   Sae large, while we're oblig'd to neither?
Our fpacious Sauls Immenfe defires,
   And ay be in a hankerin Swither.

TIBBY's Shape and Airs are fine,
And *Nelly's* Beauties are Divine;
But fince they canna baith be mine,
   Ye Gods give Ear to my Petition,
Provide a good Lad for the tane,
   But let it be with this Provifion,
I get the other to my lane,
   In Profpect *plase* and Fruition.

Up

Up in the AIR.

NOw the Sun's gane out o' Sight,
   Beet the Ingle, and snuff the Light:
In Glens the Fairies skip and dance,
And Witches wallop o'er to *France*,
      Up in the Air
       On my bonny grey Mare,
And I see her yet, and I see her yet,
    Up in, &c.

THe Wind's drifting Hail and Sna',
O'er frozen Hags like a Foot-Ba',
Nae Starns keek through the Azure Slit,
'Tis cauld and mirk as ony Pit.
     The Man i'the Moon
     Is carowsing aboon,
D'ye see, d'ye see, d'ye see him yet.
    The Man, &c.

N 2   TAKE

TAKE your Glass to clear your Een,
'Tis the Elixir heals the Spleen,
Baith Wit and Mirth it will inspire,
And gently puffs the Lover's Fire.
   Up in the Air,
    It drives away Care,
Ha'e wi'ye, ha'e wi'ye, and ha'e wi'ye
 Lads yet.
   Up in, &c.

STEEK the Doors, keep out the Frost,
Come, *Willie*, gi'es about ye'er Tost;
Til't Lads, and lilt it out,
And let us hae a blythsome Bout.
    Up wi't there, there,
     Dinna cheat, but drink fair,
HUZZA, HUZZA, and HUZZA Lads yet,
   Up wi't, &c.

F3

Fy gar rub her o'er wi' Strae.

GIN ye meet a bonny Laſſie,
 Gie 'er a Kiſs and let her gae,
But if ye meet a dirty Huſſy,
Fy gar rub her o'er wi' Strae.

BE ſure ye dinna quat the Grip
Of ilka Joy, when ye are young,
Before auld Age your Vitals nip,
And lay ye twafald o'er a Rung.

SWEET Youth's a blyth and hartſome
  Time,
Then, Lads and Laſſes, while 'tis *May*,
Gae pu' the Gowan in its Prime,
Before it wither and decay.

N 3   WATC

WATCH the faft Minutes of Delyte,
When *Jenny* fpeaks beneath her Breath,
And kiffes, laying a' the Wyte
On you, if fhe kepp ony Skaith.

HAITH ye're ill bred, fhe'll fmiling fay,
Ye'll worry me, ye greedy Rook;
Syne frae your Arms fhe'll rin away,
And hide her felf in fome dark Nook.

HER Laugh will lead you to the Place,
Where lies the Happinefs ye want,
And plainly tell you to your Face,
Nineteen Na-fays are haff a Grant.

Now to her heaving Bofom cling,
And fweetly toolie for a Kifs,
Frae her fair Finger whoop a Ring,
As Taiken of a future Blefs.

THESE Bennifons, I'm very fure,
Are of the Gods indulgent Grant;
Then, furly Carles, whifht, forbear
To plague us with your whinning Cant.

PATIE

PATIE *and* PEGGIE.

PATIE.

BY the delicious Warmnefs of thy Mouth,
  And rowing Eye, which fmiling tells
    the Truth,
I guefs, my Laffie, that, as well as I,
You're made for Love, and why fhould ye
  deny.

PEGGIE.

Bot ken ye, Lad, gin we confefs o'er foon,
Ye think us cheap, and fyne the Wooing's
    done :
The Maiden that o'er quickly tines her
    Pow'r,
Like unripe Fruit, will tafte but hard and
    fowr. .

PATIE.

But when they hing o'er lang upon
    the Tree,
Their Sweetnefs they may tine, and fae
    may ye:

Red

Red cheek'd you completely ripe appear,
And I have thol'd, and woo'd ye lang haff
   Year.

P E G G I E.

THEN dinna pu' me; gently thus I fa'
Into my *Patie*'s Arms for good and a':
But ftint your Wifhes to this frank Embrace,
And mint nae farrer till we've got the Grace.

P A T I E.

O charming Armsfou! Hence ye Cares
   away,
I'll kifs my Treafure a' the live lang Day;
A' Night I'll dream my Kiffes o'er again,
Till that Day come that ye'll be a' my ain.

C H O R U S.

Sun, gallop down the Weftlin Skyes,
Gang foon to Bed, and quickly rife,
O lafh ye'r Steeds, pafs Time away,
And hafte about our Bridal Day;
And if ye're weary'd, honeft Light,
Sleep gin ye like a Week that Night.

The

The Mill, Mill, ----O.

BENEATH a green Shade I fand a fair
　　· Maid
Was fleeping found and ftill — O,
A' lowan wi' Love my Fancy did rove,
　Around her with good Will -- O,
Her Bofom I prefs'd, but funk in her Reft
　She ftir'dna my Joy to fpill -- O:
While kindly fhe flept, clofe to her I crept,
　And kifs'd, and kifs'd her my fill — O.

OBLIG'D by Command in *Flanders* to
　　land,
　T'employ my Courage and Skill — O;
Frae'er quietly I ftaw, hoift Sails and awa',
　For Wind blew fair on the Bill --- O.
Twa Years brought me hame, where loud
　　fraifing Fame
Tald me with a Voice right fhill — O,
My Lafs like a Fool had mounted the Stool,
　Nor kend wha'd done her the Ill — O.
　　　　　　　　　　　　　　　　MAIR

Mair fond of her Charms, with my Son
    in her Arms,
  I ferlying fpear'd how fhe fell — O;
Wi' the Tear in her Eye, quoth fhe, Let
    me die,
  Sweet Sir, gin I can tell — O.
Love gave the Command, I took her by
    the Hand,
  And bade her a' Fears expell — O,
And nae mair look wan, for I was the Man
  Wha had done her the Deed my fell — O.

My bonny fweet Lafs on the gowany
    Grafs,
  Beneath the *Shilling-hill* — O,
If I did Offence, I'le make ye Amends
  Before I leave *Peggy's-Mill* — O.
O the Mill, Mill — O, and the Kill, Kill — O,
  And the cogging of the Wheel — O;
The Sack and the Sieve, a' thae ye maun
    leave,
  And round with a Sodger reel — O.
                    Colin

Colin *and* Grify *parting.*

To the Tune of, *Woe's my Heart that we should sunder.*

WITH broken Words and down-cast
       Eyes,
Poor *Colin* spoke his Paffion tender;
And parting with his *Grify,* cries,
Ah! woe's my Heart that we should fun-
    der.

To others I am cold as Snow,
But kindle with thine Eyes like Tinder;
From thee with Pain I'm forc'd to go,
It breaks my Heart that we should funder.

CHAIN'D to thy Charms I cannot range,
No Beauty new my Love fhall hinder,
Nor Time nor Place fhall ever change
My Vows, tho' we're oblig'd to funder.
              THE

THE Image of thy graceful Air,
And Beauties which invites our Wonder;
Thy lively Wit and Prudence rare
Shall still be present, tho' we sunder.

DEAR Nymph, believe thy Swain in this,
You'll ne'er engage a Heart that's kinder;
Then seal a Promise with a Kiss,
Always to love me, tho' we sunder.

YE Gods, take Care of my dear Lass,
That as I leave her I may find her:
When that blest Time shall come to pass
We'll meet again and never sunder.

The Gaberlunzie-man.

THE pauky auld Carle came o'er the Lee
Wi' many good E'ens and Days to me,
saying, Goodwife, for your Courtesie,
  Will ye lodge a silly poor Man.
The Night was cauld, the Carle was wat,
And down ayont the Ingle he sat;
My Daughter's Shoulders he 'gan to clap,
  And cadgily ranted and sang ;

O wow, quo' he, were I as free,
As first when I saw this Country,
How blyth and merry wad I be ?
  And I wad never think lang.
He grew canty, and she grew fain ;
But little did her auld Minny ken
What thir slee twa togither were say'n,
  When wooing they were sa thrang.

Ass O, quo' he, ann ye were as black,
As e'er the Crown of my Dady's Hat,
I'm I wad lay thee by my Back,
    And awa wi' me thou shou'd gang.

And O, quech she, ann I were as white,
As e'er the Snaw lay on the Dike,
I'd cleed me braw, and Lady-like,
    And awa with thee I'd gang.

※

Between the twa was made a Plot;
They raise a wee before the Cock,
And wysely they shot the Lock,
    And fast to the Bent are they gane.

Up the Morn the auld Wife raise,
And at her Leisure pat on her Claise,
Syne to the Servants Bed she gaes
    To spear for the silly poor Man.

※

She gaed to the Bed, where the Beggar lay,
The Strae was cauld, he was away,
She clapt her Hands, cry'd, Waladay,
    For some of our Gear will be gane.

                                Some

Some run to Coffers, and fome to Kifts,
But nought was ftown that cou'd be mift,
She danc'd her lane, cry'd, Praife be bleft,
   I have lodg'd a leel poor Man.

Since maithing's awa, as we can learn,
The Kirn's to kirn, and Milk to earn,
Gae butt theHoufe,Lafs,& waken my Bairn, .
   And bid her come quickly ben.
The Servant gade where the Daughter lay
The Sheets was cauld, fhe was away,
And faft to her Goodwife can fay,
   She's aff with the Gaberlunzie-man.

O fy gar ride, and fy gar rin,
And haft ye find thefe Traitors again;
For fhe's be burnt, and he's be flain
   The wearyfou Gaberlunzie man.
Some rade upo' Horfe, fome ran a fit,
The Wife was wood, and out o'er Wit;
She cou'd na gang, nor yet cou'd fhe fit,
But ay fhe curs'd and fhe ban'd.

      Mean

MEAN Time far hind out o'er the Lee,
Fou snug in a Glen where nane cou'd see,
The twa with kindly Sport and Glee,
  Cut frae a new Cheese a Whang.
The Priving was good, it pleas'd them baith,
To lo'e her for ay, he gae her his Aith.
Quo' she, to leave thee, I will be laith,
  My winsome Gaberlunzie man.

O kend my Minny I were wi' you,
Illfardly wad she crook her Mou,
Sic a poor Man she'd never trow,
  After the Gaberlunzie man.

My Dear, quo' he, ye're yet o'er young,
And ha' na learn'd the Beggars Tongue,
To follow me frae Town to Town,
  And carry the Gaberlunzie on.

Wi' Kauk and Keel, I'll win your Bread,
And Spindles & Whorles for them wha need,
Whilk is a gentle Trade indeed
  To carry the Gaberlunzie···o.

I'll

I'll bow my Leg and crook my Knee,
And draw a black Clout o'er my Eye,
A Criple or Blind they will ca' me,
   While we shall be merry and sing.

                       I.

The CORDIAL.

To the Tune of, *Where shall our Good-*
man ly.

H E.

WHERE wad bonny *Ann*ly,
   Alane nae mair ye maun ly;
Wad ye a Good-man try?
   Is that the Thing ye're laking?

S H E.

CAN a Lass sae young as I,
Venture on the Bridal Tye,
Syne down with a Good-man ly?
   I'm fleed he keep me waking.

          O 3   NEVER

H E.

Never judge until ye try,
Mak me your Goodman, I
Shanna binder you to ly,
.. And fleep till ye be weary.

S H E.

What if I fhou'd waking ly
When the Hoboys are gawn by,
Will ye tent me when I cry,
My Dear, I'm faint and iry?

H E.

In my Bofom thou fhall ly,
When thou wakrife art or dry,.
Healthy Cordial ftanding by,
Shall prefently revive thee.

S H E.

To your Will I then comply,
Join us, Prieft, and let me try
How I'll wi' a Goodman ly,
Wha can a Cordial give me.

Ew Boughts Marion.

WILL ye go to the Ew Boughts, *Marion*,
  And wear in the Sheep wi' me;
The Sun shines sweet, my *Marion*;
  But nae haf sae sweet as thee.
O *Marion*'s a bony Lass,
  And the Blyth blinks in her Eye,
And fain wad I marry *Marion*,
  Gin *Marion* wad marry me.

THERE's Gowd in your Garters, *Marion*,
  And Silk on your white Hauss-bane:
Fou fain wad I kiss my *Marion*
  At F'en when I come hame.
There's braw Lads in *Earnslaw, Marion*,
  Wha gape, and glowr with their Eye,
At Kirk when they see my *Marion*;
  But nane of them loes like me.

I've

I've nine Milk Ews, my *Marion*,
  A Cow, and a brawny Quey,
I'll gi' them a' to my *Marion*,
  Juſt on her Bridal Day;
And ye's get a green Sey-Apron,
  And Waſtcoat o' the *London* Brown,
And wow but ye will be vap'ring,
  When e'r ye gang to the Town.

I'm young and ſtout, my *Marion*,
  Nane dances like me on the Green,
And gin ye forſake me, *Marion*,
  I'll e'en gae draw up wi' *Jean* ;
Sae put on your Pearlins, Marion,
  And Cyrtle o' the Cramaſie :
And ſoon as my Chin has nae Hair on,
  I ſhall come weſt and ſee ye.

  Q.

The blythsome Bridal.

FY let us a' to the Bridal,
  For there will be Lilting there;
For *Jocky*'s to be married to *Maggie*,
  The Lass we' the Gowden Hair.
And there will be Lang-kail and Portage
  And Bannocks of Barley-meal;
And there will be good fawt Herring,
  To relish a Cog of good Ale.
Fy let us a' to the Bridal, &c.

AND there will be *Sandy* the Suter,
  And *Will* wi' the meikle Mou;
And there will be *Tam* the Blutter,
  With *Andrew* the Tinkler, I trow;
And there will be bow'd legged *Robbie*,
  With thumbless *Katie's* Goodman;
And there will be blew cheeked *Dowbie*,
  And *Lawrie* the Laird of the Land.
Fy let us, &c.

And there will be Sow libber *Pate*
  And plucky-fac't *Was* i' the Mill,
Capper nos'd *Francie*, and *Gibbie*,
  That wins in the How of the Hill;
And there will be *Alaster Sibbie*,
  Wha in with black *Beffy* did mool,
With fnivelling *Lilly* and *Tibby*,
  Th: Lafs that ftands aft on the Stool.
Fy let us, &c.

A N D *Madge* that was buckled to *Swain*,
  And coft him gray Breeks to his Arfe,
Wha after was hangit for ftealing,
  Great Mercy it hap'ned nae warfe;
And there will be gleed *Gordy Jamiefs*.
  And *Kirfb* with the Lilly whi e Leg,
Wha gade to the South for Manners
  And bang'd up her Wame in *Mons-Meg*.
Fy let us, &c.

A N D there will be *Juden M'lowrie*,
  And blinkin daft *Barbara M'leg*,
Wi' Flea-lugged, fhamy fac't *Laurie*,
  And fhangy m u'd ha'ucaet *Meg*;

                 And

And there will be Happer-ars'd *Nanfie*,
  And fairy-fac't *Floorie* by Nature,
Muck *Madie*, and fat hippit *Grify*,
  The Lafs wi' the Gowden Watte.
Fy let us, &c.

And there will be *Girn-again-Gibby*,
  With his glakit Wife *Jenny Bell*,
And Mifle-fhin'd *Mango M'capie*,
  The Lad that was Skipper himfel.
There Lads and Laffes in Pearlings
  Will feaft in the Heart of the Ha,
On Sybows, and Rifarts, and Carlings
  That are baith fodden and raw.
Fy let us, &c.

And there will be Fadges and Brachen,
  With Fouth of good Gabbocks of Skate,
Powfowdie, and Drammock and Crowdie,
  And caller Nowt-feet in a Plate ;
And there will be Partans and Buckies,
  And Whytens and Speldings enew,
With finged Sheep-heads, and a Haggies,
And Scadlips to fup till ye fpew.
Fy let us, &c.   And

AND there will be lapper'd Milk Kebbucks,
 And Sowens, and Farles, and Baps,
With Swats, and well scraped Paunches,
 And Brandy in Stoups and in Caps ;
And there will be Meal-kail and Castocks
 With Skink to sup till ye rive,
And Roasts to roast on a Brander,
 Of Flowks that were taken alive.
Fy let us, &c.

SCRAPT Haddocks, Wilks, Dulse and Tangle,
 And a Mill of good Snishing to prie;
When weary with Eating and Drinking,
 Well rise up and dance till we die.
Then fy let us a' to the Bridal,
 For there will be Lilting there,
For Jocky's to be married to Maggie,
 The Lass wi' the gowden Hair.

       Z.

The Highland Laddie.

THE Lawland Lads think they are fine,
  But O they'r vain and idly gaudy!
How much unlike that gracefu' Mein,
  And manly Looks of my HighlandLaddie?
O my bonny bonny Highland Laddie,
My handsome charming Highland Laddie:
May Heaven still guard, and Love reward
Our Lawland Lass and her Highland Laddie.

If I were free at Will to chuse
  To be the wealthiest Lawland Lady,
I'd take young Donald without Trews,
  With Bonnet blew and belted Plaidy.
O my bonny, &c.

THe bravest Beau in Borrows-Town,
  In a' his Airs, with Art made ready,
Compard to him, he's but a Clown;
  He's finer far in's Tartan Plaidy.
  O my bonny, &c.

P   O'ER

O'er benty Hill with him I'll run,
   And leave my Lawland Kin and Dady.
Frae Winter's Canld and Summer's Sun,
   He'll screen me with his Highland Plaidy.
O my bonny, &c.

A painted Room and Silken Bed,
   May please a Lawland Laird and Lady;
But I can kifs and be as glad
   Behind a Bush in's Highland Plaidy.
O my bonny, &c.

Few Compliments between us pafs,
   I ca' him my dear Highland Laddie,
And he ca's me his Lawland Lafs;
   Syne rows me in beneath his Plaidy.
O my bonny &c.

Nae greater Joy I'll e'er pretend,
   Than that his Love prove true and steady
Like mine to him, which ne'er shall end,
   While Heaven preserves my Highland
      Laddie.
O my bonny &c.

                                             Allan

ALLAN-WATER.

Or, *My Love* Annie's *very bonny.*

WHAT Numbers shall the Muse repete?
What Verse be found to praise
  my *Annie?*
On her ten thousand Graces wait,
  Each Swain admires, and owns she's bonny.
Since first she trode the happy Plain,
  She set each youthful Heart on Fire,
Each Nymph does to her Swain complain,
  That *Annie* kindles new Desire.

THIS lovely Darling dearest Care;
  This new Delight, this charming *Annie,*
Like Summer's Dawn, she's fresh and fair,
  When *Flora's* fragrant Breezes fan ye.
All Day the am'rous Youths conveen,
  Joyous they sport and play before her;
All Night, when she no more is seen,
  In blessful Dreams they still adore her.

AMONG

Among the Crowd *Amyntor* came,
  He look'd, he loov'd, he bow'd to *Annie*;
His rising Sighs express his Flame,
  His Words were few, his Wishes many.
With Smiles the lovely Maid replied,
  Kind Shepherd why should I deceive ye?
Alas! your Love must be deny'd,
  This destin'd Breast can ne'er relieve ye.

Young *Damon* came, with *Cupid*'s Art,
  His Wiles, his Smiles, his Charms be-
    guiling,
He stole away my Virgin-Heart,
  Cease, poor *Amyntor*, cease bewailing.
Some brighter Beauty you may find,
  On yonder Plain the Nymphs are many,
Then chuse some Heart that's unconfin'd,
  And serve to *Damon* his own *Annie*.
                                    C.

The Collier's bonny Lassie.

THE Collier has a Daughter,
  And O she's wonder bonny,
A Laird he was that sought her,
  Rich baith in Land and Money;
The Tutors watch'd the Motion
  Of this young honest Lover,
But Love is like the Ocean:
  Wha can its Depth discover?

HE had the Art to please ye,
  And was by a' respected;
His Airs sat round him easy,
  Genteel, but unaffected.
The Collier's bonny Lassie
  Fair as the new blown Lillie,
Ay sweet, and never saucy,
  Secur'd the Heart of *Willy*.

Ha

He lov'd beyond Expreſſion,
  The Charms that were about her,
And panted for Poſſeſſion,
  His Life was dull without her.
After mature reſolving,
  Cloſs to his Breaſt he held her,
In ſafteſt Flames diſſolving,
  He tenderly thus tell'd her.

My bonny Collier's Daughter,
  . Let naething diſcompoſe ye,
'Tis no your ſcanty Tocher
  Shall ever gar me loſe ye;
For I have Gear in Plenty,
  And Love ſays, 'tis my Duty
To ware what Heaven has lent me,
  Upon your Wit and Beauty.

Where

Where HELEN *lies.*

TO——in Mourning.

AH why thefe Tears in *Nellie*'s Eyes,
   To hear thy tender Sighs and Cries,
The Gods ftand lift'ning from the Skies
   Pleas'd with thy Piety.
To mourn the Dead, dear Nymph, forbear,
   And of one dying take a Care,
Who views thee as an Angel fair,
      Or fome Divinity.

O be lefs graceful or more kind,
And cool this Fever of my Mind,
Caufed by the Boy fevere and blind,
      Wounded I figh for thee;
                                    While

While hardly dare I hope to rise
To such a Height by *Hymen's* Tyes,
To lay me down where *Helen* lyes
　　And with thy Charms be free.

THEN must I hide my Love and die,
When such a sovereign Cure is by?
No, she can love, and I'll go try,
　　Whate're my Fate may be,
Which soon I'll read in her bright Eyes,
With those dear Agents I'll advise, (Lies,
They tell the Truth, when Tongues tell
　　The least believ'd by me.

CON-

SONG.

To the Tune of *Gallowshiels*.

'AH the Shepherd's mournful Fate,
    When doom'd to love, and doom'd
      to languish,
To bear the scornful fair one's Hate,
    Nor dare disclose his Anguish.
Yet eager Looks, and dying Sighs,
    My secret Soul discovers;
While Rapture trembling thro' my Eyes,
    Reveals how much I love her.
The tender Glance, the redning Cheek,
    O'erspread with rising Blushes,
A thousand various Ways they speak
    A thousand various Wishes.

                     For

For Oh! that Form fo heavenly fair,
   Thofe languid Eyes fo fweetly fmiling,
That artlefs Blufh and modeft Air,
   So fatally beguiling.
Thy every Look, and every Grace,
   So charm when e'er I view thee,
Till Death o'ertake me in the Chace,
   Still will my Hopes purfue thee;
Then when my tedious Hours are paft,
   Be this laft Bleffing given,
Low at thy Foot to breath my laft,
   And die in Sight of Heaven.

By Wm. Hamilton of Bangour.

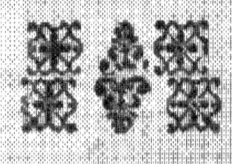

CON-

CONTENTS

The following marked C, D, H, L, M, O, &c. are new Words by different Hands, X, the Authors unknown; Z, old Songs; Q. old Songs with Additions.

Page.

The

Gilbert.

CONTENTS. 181

---

*The following without a Mark, the Words
by* Allan Ramfay.

CONTENTS.

F I N I S.